This month, in **SECRET AGENT DAD**
by Metsy Hingle, meet Blake Hunt—
debonair secret agent. Disguised as a father of
twins, Blake was not prepared for
Josie Walters—a beautiful country widow who
wants to be a mother to those two precious babies!

**SILHOUETTE DESIRE
IS PROUD TO PRESENT THE**

Five wealthy Texas bachelors—all members of
the state's most exclusive club—set out on a
mission to rescue a princess...and find true love.

* * *

And don't miss LONE STAR PRINCE
by Cindy Gerard, the final installment of the
Texas Cattleman's Club, available next month in
Silhouette Desire!

Dear Reader,

Hey, look us over—our brand-new cover makes Silhouette Desire look more desirable than ever! And between the covers we're continuing to offer those powerful, passionate and provocative love stories featuring rugged heroes and spirited heroines.

Mary Lynn Baxter returns to Desire and locates our November MAN OF THE MONTH in the *Heart of Texas*, where a virgin heroine is wary of involvement with a younger man.

More heart-pounding excitement can be found in the next installment of the Desire miniseries TEXAS CATTLEMAN'S CLUB with *Secret Agent Dad* by Metsy Hingle. Undercover agent Blake Hunt loses his memory but gains adorable twin babies—and the heart of lovely widow Josie Walters!

Ever-popular Dixie Browning presents a romance in which opposites attract in *The Bride-in-Law*. Elizabeth Bevarly offers you *A Doctor in Her Stocking*, another entertaining story in her miniseries FROM HERE TO MATERNITY. *The Daddy Search* is Shawna Delacorte's story of a woman's search for the man she believes fathered her late sister's child. And a hero and heroine are in jeopardy on an island paradise in Kathleen Korbel's *Sail Away*.

Each and every month, Silhouette Desire offers you six exhilarating journeys into the seductive world of romance. So make a commitment to sensual love and treat yourself to all six!

Enjoy!

Joan Marlow Golan
Senior Editor, Silhouette Desire

Please address questions and book requests to:
Silhouette Reader Service
U.S.: 3010 Walden Ave., P.O. Box 1325, Buffalo, NY 14269
Canadian: P.O. Box 609, Fort Erie, Ont. L2A 5X3

Secret Agent Dad
METSY HINGLE

Published by Silhouette Books
America's Publisher of Contemporary Romance

To the four talented authors with whom I've had the
privilege of sharing this series—Dixie Browning,
Caroline Cross, Cindy Gerard and Peggy Moreland—
and for the brave editor who directed us all:
Karen Kosztolnyik

Special thanks and acknowledgment are given
to Metsy Hingle for her contribution to the
Texas Cattleman's Club series.

SILHOUETTE BOOKS

ISBN 0-373-76250-X

SECRET AGENT DAD

Copyright © 1999 by Harlequin Books S.A.

All rights reserved. Except for use in any review, the reproduction
or utilization of this work in whole or in part in any form by any
electronic, mechanical or other means, now known or hereafter
invented, including xerography, photocopying and recording, or in
any information storage or retrieval system, is forbidden without
the written permission of the editorial office, Silhouette Books,
300 East 42nd Street, New York, NY 10017 U.S.A.

All characters in this book have no existence outside the imagination of
the author and have no relation whatsoever to anyone bearing the same
name or names. They are not even distantly inspired by any individual
known or unknown to the author, and all incidents are pure invention.

This edition published by arrangement with Harlequin Books S.A.

® and TM are trademarks of Harlequin Books S.A., used under license.
Trademarks indicated with ® are registered in the United States Patent
and Trademark Office, the Canadian Trade Marks Office and in other
countries.

Visit us at www.romance.net

Printed in U.S.A.

Books by Metsy Hingle

Silhouette Desire

Seduced #900
Surrender #978
Backfire #1026
Lovechild #1055
The Kidnapped Bride #1103
Switched at the Altar #1133
The Bodyguard and the Bridesmaid #1146
Dad in Demand #1241
Secret Agent Dad #1250

*Right Bride, Wrong Groom

METSY HINGLE

is an award-winning, bestselling author of romance who resides across the lake from her native New Orleans. Married for more than twenty years to her own hero, she is the busy mother of four children. She recently traded in her business suits and a fast-paced life in the hotel and public relations arena to pursue writing full-time. Metsy has a strong belief in the power of love and romance. She also believes in happy endings, which she continues to demonstrate with each new story she writes. She loves hearing from readers. Write to Metsy at P.O. Box 3224, Covington, LA 70433.

"What's Happening in Royal?"

NEWS FLASH, November 1999—Who could have predicted that a storm the size of our Lone Star State would blow into these parts with such vengeance? Never has the town of Royal seen such theatrics as the thunder-'n'-lightnin' show put on by good ole Mother Nature. Power lines knocked out…roads aplenty closed down. The Royal Diner is especially concerned about that lovely widow Josie Walters, who left the diner in her pickup the day of the storm on her way back to her farm—she's quite a woman to be running things all on her own out there in the middle of nowhere!

Royal is also buzzing regarding the whereabouts of Blake Hunt, the man of mystery and dashing younger brother of hotshot attorney Gregory Hunt. Seems his older brother has been seen about town fraught with worry.…

And rumors are flying about a possible "royal" sighting of the formidable Prince Ivan Striksy. Could our Texas Cattleman's Club members be entertaining this princely visitor…or keeping him under wraps? Our sources will tell you soon!

Prologue

The blood in Blake Hunt's veins chilled at the sound of a baby's whimper coming from the backseat of his car. He'd learned a major lesson in the past forty-eight hours—bachelors and babies did not mix. Given a choice, he'd rather face a firing squad than the four-month-old twins strapped in the seats behind him.

"Why couldn't I get a simple assignment—like disarming a band of terrorists?" Pressing one booted foot to the accelerator, he sent the sedan speeding down the dark Texas road, barely visible in the heavy rainstorm courtesy of La Niña.

Bone tired from the mission he'd undertaken on behalf of the Alpha Team and his brother Greg, Blake replayed the escape from the palace in his head. Even with his training as a former Cobra, getting the royal twins out of the tiny principality of Asterland where they had been held hostage had not been an easy task. But he'd done it. He'd rescued the motherless babies and thwarted Prince Ivan's plans to use them in his plot to gain control of the kingdom of Oberland.

And in less than two hours, weather permitting, his end of the mission would be completed. They would be in Royal, Texas, and he would gladly turn the pair over to their aunt.

Another whimper cut through his musings. Despite the November cold, sweat beaded across his brow. He lifted his gaze heavenward. Please. Don't let them wake up again. The whimper escalated to a wail. "So much for prayers," he muttered.

"Hang on a second, sugar britches," he soothed, dividing his attention between the blue-eyed babies seated behind him and the storm-ravaged road stretched out before him. He negotiated the sedan around another curve and swore as a fist of wind came at him and nearly tossed them off the road. Gripping the steering wheel, Blake fought to steady the car while he braced himself for the second baby to join its twin's protests. As if on cue the other baby began to howl, and the wails continued in chorus. Blake still didn't know which was worse—the nerve-wrenching cries of the twins or driving through the worst rainstorm to hit West Texas since Noah had piloted his ark.

Sighing, he darted another glance at the healthy-lunged duo seated behind him. An unexpected warmth spread through him as he looked at the tiny pair all bundled up in the ugly camouflage jackets he'd put on them in their escape from the palace. Miranda—he was sure it had to be that future heartbreaker—stretched out her little arms toward him.

Blake's heart did a nosedive.

"Shh. It's okay, sugar. Uncle Blake's here." Unfastening his seat belt, he stretched one arm behind him to stroke her tiny hands with his finger. Despite the contact, she continued to sob. And each one of those pitiful sobs ripped right through him. Nearly frantic, he tried to think what to do. "Pacifiers!" Groping in the diaper bag on the seat beside him, his fingers closed around a rubber nipple. "Here you go," he said, managing to pop it in her mouth.

He was debating whether to stop and get the other nipple

for Edward, when the baby stopped crying, and started to doze off. Relieved, Blake directed his attention back to the road and frowned. The weather appeared to be worse now than when he'd started out from the airport where he'd landed his plane earlier. The usually dry gullies were filling rapidly. Never once in his thirty years could he remember weather like this in West Texas. But he couldn't stop and wait for it to blow over. He had to get home—to Royal—tonight. His brother Greg and the Alpha Team, all members of the exclusive Texas Cattleman's Club, were counting on him. So was Princess Anna.

Another glance at the backseat revealed the twosome were asleep. Anger twisted inside him as he thought about Prince Ivan and his attempts to use them. From what he'd learned of the man, the prince would not be a gracious loser. "Don't you two worry. Uncle Blake won't let him get anywhere near you again. I promise."

Rain pummeled the car like fists, making it nearly impossible to see the road. The windshield wipers worked furiously, offering him only split-second views of the road. His thoughts still on the prince, Blake didn't see the shattered arm of a windmill in the road until he was almost on top of it. He whipped the wheel to his left, just missing it. Struggling to maintain control, he began applying the brakes. A blast of wind slapped at the car from behind and sent the sedan skidding sideways across the road. Blake fought to keep the car from flipping over, but there was no way to avoid hitting the low bridge over the creek. He slammed into the railing, and the car pivoted and began skidding down the shoulder. The babies screamed. Blake lurched forward, cracking his head against the windshield before the car came to a halt.

Dazed, blood trickling down his forehead, the frightened cries of the babies pierced his fogged senses. The twins! He had to get the twins. Fighting pain and the darkness that threatened to engulf him, Blake shoved against the door. It

opened, and he fell to his knees in mud and water. He tried
to stand, but the wind slammed him back against the car. His
head struck the door, and pain exploded in his skull. His
vision blurred. Clutching his head in his hands, he slumped
to the ground, unaware of his wallet falling beside him, of
the wind tossing the black billfold down toward the creek
and into the rushing water.

And as the rain beat down over him, Blake succumbed to
the beckoning darkness.

One

Stupid. Stupid. Stupid.

Josie Walters smacked her fist against the steering wheel of her aging Explorer and glared at the windshield wipers as they waged a losing battle with the punishing rain. Slowing to little more than a crawl, she pointed the blue truck down the dark, empty road. "I should never have waited so long to leave Royal," she grumbled.

She should have been home hours ago, safe and warm in her farmhouse, not driving through this monster-size storm. And she would have been, if she hadn't listened to that Pollyanna voice in her head again.

"What made me think that placing an ad for a farmhand would be the answer to my prayers? Some answer!" Clenching the steering wheel with her fingers, Josie mocked her own foolish optimism.

"You're a first-rate idiot, Josie Walters." Because only an idiot would have convinced herself to wait for that last job applicant, believing he would be any different from the other five men she'd interviewed and ruled out. Not only had number six, a drifter named Pete Mitchell, been just as incapable and overpriced as the others, but the man had actually expected access to her bed as a fringe benefit.

"The jerk! Sex-starved widow, indeed!" Remembering the remark, she fumed, and prayed that Forrest Cunningham, a member of that ritzy Texas Cattleman's Club, hadn't overheard him. Everyone else in the diner probably had, though. How would she ever be able to set foot in Royal again? The fact that she'd even allowed the beady-eyed excuse for a man to finish making the proposition with his hand on her rear end before she'd dumped her coffee in his lap proved what a desperate fool she was. At the admission, some of the fight went out of her, and she sighed.

When will you learn, Josie? You are not *Cinderella. Not even close. Didn't all those years of being passed over for adoption teach you that much? If you had any doubts, surely that cheating man you married hammered home the message. After all, it wasn't* you *he'd taken with him to Dallas when he wrapped his car around that utility pole. You didn't quite measure up, remember? That's why he'd taken that pretty new waitress from Midland with him. Face it, Josie girl. The only fairy-tale endings or princes you're likely to find are between the covers of a book.*

Pushing the painful memories aside, Josie focused on today's blunder while she continued to creep down the road. Not only was she out the cost of the ad, she'd also lost another day. A day she could ill afford to lose when so much work still needed to be done before the bank's inspection. How was she supposed to get the farm in shape if she couldn't find help that she could afford? And what would she do if the bank turned down her request for a loan and she lost the farm?

Acid churned in Josie's stomach at the thought. She wouldn't lose the farm. She couldn't. Regardless of her disaster of a marriage, at least Ben had left her the farm. And despite its run-down condition, the place was her home. Home. For the first time in her twenty-nine years she actually had one she could call her own. And she wasn't about to give it up without a fight. Somehow, some way, she would find a way to keep it with or without the loan. She had to.

Suddenly a speed limit sign flew into her path, and Josie swerved to miss it. Her heart slamming in her chest, she pulled onto the shoulder of the road and noted for the first time that the storm was getting worse. When she'd left Royal there had only been a stiff wind. But now sheets of rain had joined the howling wind, whipping across the landscape and her truck. Josie shivered and turned up the collar of her denim jacket. Maybe she'd be wise to shelve her worries about the farm for the time being and concentrate on getting home in one piece.

Shifting the truck out of Park, she carefully eased it back onto the road. She'd never seen weather like this before—not in this part of Texas, where rain was such a rarity. Thinking back on how often she'd wished for rain for her roses, Josie shook her head. She certainly had never wanted anything like this…this deluge. She could handle the occasional sandstorms common to the area, but she didn't have a clue on how to deal with a flood. Suddenly nerves twisted like knots in her stomach, because judging by the amount of water already in the normally dry creek bed, she could very well be facing a flood by morning unless this stopped.

Leaning forward to peer through the windshield, Josie tried to see the road between the swipes of the windshield wipers. Up ahead she could make out the arm of a windmill lying smashed in the middle of the road. A prickle of uneasiness skipped down her spine.

As she approached the broken windmill blade, a glimmer of light to the left caught her eye. Her heartbeat tripled at the sight of a car pointed nose down toward the rising creek bed. Then she spied a body sprawled next to it. "Oh, my God!"

Pulling her Explorer off to the side of the road, Josie set the emergency brake and quickly released her seat belt.

Not bothering with an umbrella or slicker, she shoved open the truck's door and broke into a run down the incline toward the wrecked car. Before she'd gone three feet, she was soaked to the skin and shivering from the cold. Slapping hair out of her eyes, Josie clamped her chattering teeth together and dropped down beside the man's body. Her heart pounded like a jackhammer as she pressed her fingers to the pulse in his neck. Relief shot through her when she found it strong and steady.

"Can you hear me?" she yelled to be heard above the wind. When he moaned, she tilted his head toward the light shining down from her truck. Josie's breath caught as she saw him. Oh my. What a face. The face of a golden prince. High cheekbones, sharp jaw, sexy mouth. Even unconscious and with a nasty cut on his forehead, the man would make grown women drool. He stirred, moaned again, then his eyelids fluttered. Brown eyes with flecks of gold stared up at her.

"Wh-what happened?" he asked, his voice as rough as sandpaper and barely audible above the roar of wind.

"You've had an accident," she fairly shouted, trying to make herself heard. Although the rain seemed to slacken, the wind had picked up considerably. "You must have hit that broken windmill blade in the road. Judging by that nasty cut on your forehead, you probably hit the windshield." She glanced over at his car, then back at him. "It's a wonder the air bag didn't inflate," she said and wondered if he had disconnected it.

He looked at her as though he didn't have a clue what she was talking about. Then he lifted his hand to her face.

The unexpected touch of his fingers on her face sent a shock through Josie. Her stomach tightened. She wasn't used to being touched—especially by a man, and it had been a long time since she'd responded so strongly to a man. Ben's philandering and his catalog of her shortcomings had long ago killed any secret cravings she had to be touched by a man. An hour before she would have sworn that that part of her femininity had died long before her husband had. Evidently she'd been wrong, because her skin tingled where he'd touched her. Feeling foolish and embarrassed by her thoughts, she began checking him for other injuries.

"Wh-who are you?" he asked.

"I'm Josie. Josie Walters."

"I didn't know angels had last names."

Josie's hands stilled on his ribs. She shot her gaze back to his face. "I'm not an angel," she told him.

"Are you sure?"

"Positive," she assured him.

"I always pictured angels with eyes like yours—the color of summer grass."

The conversation was absurd, Josie told herself. She was kneeling on the side of the road in a storm with an accident victim discussing the color of her eyes. Still, she couldn't stop that fluttery sensation in her stomach. Noting the way he was watching her, she swallowed. She had to be imagining things, Josie told herself. Men didn't look at her like that. Most men didn't even look twice—at least not men like this one. There were too many beautiful women in Texas to settle for one with skinny curves, unruly hair and a forgettable face. Evidently the bump on the fellow's head had affected his eyesight. "Sorry to disappoint you, cowboy, but I'm no angel."

"I guess that means that I'm not dead, then."

Josie bit back a smile. She swiped the sopping hair from her eyes again. "Nope. You're not dead. And as far as I can tell, you don't have any broken bones, either." Still kneeling, she sat back on her heels. "You've got a few bruises and a knot the size of a lemon on the back of your head. But that cut on your forehead looks like it's going to need stitching. Do you think you can sit up?"

"Yeah."

She slipped one arm behind his neck and eased him up to a sitting position. As she did so, her breast brushed his arm. A flicker of heat licked through her at the innocent contact. Surprised and confused by her reaction, Josie bit back the urge to jerk away. But as soon as he was sitting up on his own, she dropped her arm and eased back a fraction. "Even if your car will still run, I don't think you're in any condition to drive. My truck's parked up there on the road." She motioned to where she had left the Explorer running with the lights on. "I'm no lightweight, but I doubt that I can carry you. Do you think if I help you that you can make it up to my truck? We need to get you to a hospital."

The dazed look in his eyes cleared for a moment, then sharpened. A fierce scowl transformed his face from the *GQ* label she'd pegged him with, to someone dangerous, untamed, a man who defied any label. His response to her was quick and razor edged, but it was lost in another rush of wind.

"What?" she asked, leaning closer.

"No hospitals."

"But your head—"

As though he'd forgotten the injury, he pressed his fingers to his forehead. They came away with blood, which the rain quickly washed away. When he looked up at her again, a frown lined his brow. "I'll be okay. No hospitals."

"But you're hurt."

His dark eyes grew clouded. He looked confused for a moment, then the *GQ* pinup was back. A lopsided grin curved his lips. "Just a scratch," he insisted. "I bet a kiss would make it all better."

Josie blinked rain from her eyes. Her stomach dipped. "You're crazy," she told him and started to stand.

His hand shot out and he captured her wrist. Before she could stop him, he tugged her toward him, and sent them both toppling back to the muddy ground. Then his mouth—that wet, sexy mouth of his was covering her own—kissing her with a skill and a gentleness that made Josie's head spin. She forgot about the rain. She forgot about the cold. She forgot about the fact that she was on the side of a deserted road sprawled atop a stranger—an injured stranger—with the eyes of a dark angel who kissed like a fairy-tale prince.

Suddenly, as though by magic, the wind's angry hiss lost some of its bite. Even the rain slowed. And that's when she heard it. A baby crying—crying at the top of its lungs. The sound slashed through Josie's kiss-dulled senses like a scalpel. She jerked her mouth free and scrambled back from him quicker than a snap. She gave her head a shake to clear it. Lord, now she was imagining she heard babies.

"I was right. I don't need a hospital after all. All I needed was a kiss. I'm feeling a lot better," he told her, pushing himself up to his elbows as though he were stretched out on a couch and not on the side of a road in mud.

Feeling foolish for her reaction to him, she shoved herself to her feet. "Obviously, you're not hurt as badly as I thought."

Turning her back on him, she started for her truck. Then she heard it again—a baby crying. She stopped, looked back. "This is going to sound crazy, but—"

He was right where she'd left him—only now he was lying flat on his back, his eyes closed. She hurried over to him, discovered him out cold. And once again she heard the baby crying—only this time it was louder. Pushing to her feet, Josie stepped past the unconscious stranger and headed for his wrecked car. Her boots slid in the mud as she sought purchase on the incline where the car rested at an angle. He'd shut off the engine, but the lights were still on, and the driver's door was slightly ajar.

Flinging her braid back from her face, Josie yanked open the rear door of the fancy sedan. "Oh, my God," she whispered at the sight of the two red-faced, squealing infants strapped into car seats. One of the babies held out its little arms and hands toward her as though pleading to be picked up.

A fist closed around Josie's heart. Her brain shut down, and her heart took over. "Shh. It's okay, precious," she murmured. Ducking inside the car, she released the latch on the car seat nearest to her and took the first little one into her arms. She held the baby against her breast, smoothed her fingers over the tufts of blond hair and stroked the tiny back. Almost at once the baby's sobs lessened and a tiny thumb went into its mouth.

The other baby continued to wail brokenheartedly. "It's okay. It's okay. I'm not going to leave you, sweetie." She leaned over the seat to stroke the other baby's cheek, and planted a kiss on its little fingers. Then, pulling the jacket hood up over the head of the baby she held, Josie shifted the bundle to her left shoulder and used her free hand to grab its car seat. "I'll be right back," she promised the other sobbing infant. As much as she hated to leave the remaining baby alone for even a second, she didn't dare try to take them both at once and risk falling. Shielding the baby with her body as best she could, Josie headed for her truck.

Three trips later, she had both babies strapped in the rear seat of her Explorer, relatively content with the pacifiers she'd found. The matching diaper bags and a tote with enough diapers, baby food and formula to last several weeks had been stowed safely on the back floor. All she had to do now was get their still-unconscious daddy into her truck.

Any thoughts she'd had about leaving him and going home to call for help went out the window after she discovered the babies. Opening the vial of smelling salts she'd retrieved from her truck's first-aid kit, she waved it under his nose.

He grunted, slapped the bottle away and grabbed her wrist in a paralyzing grip. His strength surprised her, given the fact that he'd been unconscious. But it was the deadly glitter in his eyes that made her heart race. "Hey, it's okay. It's me. Josie Walters. Remember?"

"Josie?" he repeated, his expression wary.

"Yes. You had an accident. Remember? I stopped to help. I need to get you out of the rain. My truck's just up there on the road. Can you stand up?"

He didn't say anything, but allowed her to help him to his feet. "That's it. Just lean on me," she told him. What seemed an eternity later, she had him in the front seat of her truck. She'd no sooner gotten him strapped in before he passed out again.

The stretch of road that normally took her fifteen minutes to drive took a full thirty as she was forced to maneuver past fallen trees, signs and a road slick with mud and rain. When she finally pulled up to her farmhouse, Josie nearly wept at the welcoming sight of the lights burning inside.

She cut off the truck's engine and flexed her fingers, positive that she'd left dents in the steering wheel during the harrowing drive. "We're home," she told the sleepy-eyed duo in the backseat. Unfastening her seat belt, she braced herself for the cool air and opened the door.

Blake felt the cool air swirl around him and tried to fight his way up from the darkness. Tossing and turning, he struggled toward the sound of a woman's soft voice. But try as he might, other voices intruded, pulled him back into the dark...back into a long, dark hall of marbled floors and foreign scents....

Hurry.

The word was a chant in his blood as Blake removed his arm from around the guard's throat. The man's body slid to the floor unconscious. Hurry. Have to hurry, Blake thought. Stepping over the guard, he made his way down the long, shadowed corridor, his feet moving silently along the polished surface. Nothing could go wrong, he told himself. Too many people were depending on him. He had studied the layout of the palace, memorized every detail, down to the position of each monarch's portrait that had lined these walls since the sixteenth century. Even in the deep shadows, he knew ten feet to his left the Asterland coat of arms hung beside the door that led to the royal nursery. He moved silently, quickly, as he had been trained to do, and took out the two guards stationed outside the door. Removing the specialized set of picks from his wallet, he inserted them into the lock. Moments later the tumblers clicked, and Blake stepped inside the room.

A check of the nanny's quarters revealed the old dragon was out cold, a snore whistling through her wrinkled lips. A smile curved his mouth as he thought of his friend wooing the lady. He'd have to remember to send Pierre an extra hundred francs as a bonus for combat pay. Romancing the woman in order to slip the drug into her wine could not have been an easy task for his friend, who preferred sleek beauties with large breasts.

Exiting the nanny's suite, he stepped inside the room of her two charges. A sliver of moonlight fought through the balcony doors, illuminating the two cribs. Nerves were bunched like fists in his gut at the task before him, but the adrenaline rush that he experienced with any mission had him heading for the balcony doors. He flicked open the locks, and without waiting to see who entered, he started toward the cribs. He hesitated at the tiny sleeping bundles. A live grenade he could handle. But a baby? What if he dropped it? What if...

"Hurry, mon ami."

The other man's voice spurred him to action. The baby didn't so much as flutter an eyelash as he wrapped it up and eased it into the pouch strapped to his chest. When he went to retrieve the other one, big blue eyes stared up at him. "Hey, sugar britches. Uncle Blake's going to take you on a trip to see your Aunt Anna. How would you like that?" The little one didn't protest, merely reached out tiny fingers to touch his black-sooted face. Blake's throat went dry. He

*caught the little hand, not wanting to dirty those perfect white
fingers with a warrior's paint.*

"Blake," the other man spit out his name in warning.
"There's something going on downstairs. Guards are rushing inside the palace."

Steps sounded outside in the corridor. Deciding quickly,
he unstrapped the pouches from his chest and began fasten-
ing them to the other man's body. "Take them to the boat."

"Are you crazy? I know nothing of babies."

"Neither do I," Blake informed his companion as he urged
him to the balcony doors.

"What if they cry?" the other man asked, his dark eyes
wide with fear and his accent more pronounced.

"Try singing to them. You always say the ladies love your
voice."

The other man grumbled something in his native tongue,
which Blake made no attempt to translate in his head. Grateful that neither baby protested this middle-of-the-night intru-
sion, he pressed a kiss to each tiny head. "Be good for
Michel. I'll see you in a little while."

"But, Blake—"

"Go," Blake ordered.

"Hurry, mon ami."

Hurry. Hurry.

The words came at him again from out of a fog—this one
of blinding rain and skidding tires. His head hurt, felt like it
was ready to explode any minute. He swiped at his head, and
groaned at another stab of pain. He could feel something
warm and sticky on his fingertips. Blood, Blake realized.
Doesn't matter. Have to keep moving.

He couldn't see. The road was too dark, the rain too strong.
And he was tired. So tired. But he couldn't stop, didn't dare
stop or they'd find him, kill him, steal the babies. He couldn't
let that happen. Only his head hurt something fierce, and he
couldn't seem to remember which way to turn.

Remember, we're depending on you, Blake. Be careful, and for God's sake man, hurry.

Blake heard the man's voice, and he struggled to sit up. "Have to hurry. Can't let them down. Gave my word," he muttered.

"Shh. It's okay." Gentle hands pressed him back down to the bed. "You can't go anywhere right now. You need to rest."

Blake tried to open his eyes, to see the face that went with the new voice that came to him out of the fog. But try as he might, his eyes refused to obey. He tried to sit up again, but was pressed back against the mattress.

"It's storming outside, and the phone lines are down," she told him. "Even if the roads are still passable, you're in no condition to drive. So, you might as well quit fighting me and try to rest." Fingers as soft and warm as the voice stroked his brow, eased the ache in his head.

"If you're worried about your babies, you don't need to be. They're safe and sound asleep in the next room."

Babies? He didn't have any babies.

He wanted to tell her that, tried to make sense of what she was saying to him, but it hurt too much when he tried to think. Instead, he allowed himself to be soothed by the gentle touch of her fingers, the sweet sound of her voice.

"Yes. That's it. Try to rest," she murmured. "I'm afraid that I'll have to wake you up again in an hour. That's what the book says to do for head injuries. Wake up the injured party every hour so that you don't go into a coma."

Talk of head injuries, comas and babies jumbled in his brain. So he focused on her touch, the soothing sound of her voice. Her familiar voice. Frowning, he tried to remember. Was she friend or enemy? Could she be trusted? When she started to press something cold against his head, he grabbed her hand.

"It's all right," she murmured, but made no attempt to

wrestle free. "You pulled the bandage loose. I'm just putting more ointment on that cut before I bandage it up again."

The need to see her, to see the face that went with the voice was so strong he battled to open his eyes. When he finally managed to do so, he caught a glimpse of familiar green eyes. "Angel," he whispered, his eyes closing again. But even as the darkness began to tug him under, he could still see those clear green eyes—the eyes of his angel.

Two

You're a good girl, Jocelyn. Not everyone can be counted on to remain calm and clearheaded in a crisis.

The crisp tone of Sister Charles Marie's voice came back to Josie as though it were only yesterday and not twenty years ago that she'd snuffed out a grease fire in the kitchen of the orphanage and saved another girl from being badly burned.

Today had been another crisis, Josie realized, as she tamed her thick, black hair into a braid. She'd remained calm and clearheaded while she'd settled the twins into the spare bedroom. She'd even managed to remain calm and clearheaded when she'd maneuvered the little darlings' daddy to the only other room with a bed—her own. And somehow, she'd managed to stay fairly calm and clearheaded when the man had started thrashing about on the bed and pulled his bandage free. But there had been nothing calm or clearheaded about the way she'd felt when he'd opened his eyes and called her "angel" again before passing out. No one had ever called her by a pet name before—certainly no one from the orphanage or the foster homes she'd lived in. To them she'd always been Jocelyn, and even Ben had never strayed from the "Josie" she'd insisted on being called. She'd come to accept the fact that she wasn't the sort of person that people called "sweetie" or "honey" or "sugar." Deep down she'd sometimes wondered if it was because she simply wasn't special enough to warrant such an endearment.

But *he* had called her "angel." Not once, but twice. It was ridiculous that his doing so should make her pulse quicken or make her feel like her heart was smiling. After all, the man had been injured, and in his delirious state he probably thought she was someone else. Yet he had looked at her the way a man looks at a woman—with appreciation, with interest—and for those few seconds awareness had hummed between them and lingered like the scent of her roses. By the time she'd repaired his bandage, she'd been too flustered to even attempt to rid him of his wet clothes.

Now, having had the benefit of a hot shower and a change of clothes herself, guilt sneaked in on her. She really shouldn't have left him in those wet things, she conceded, then groaned. "I didn't even take off his boots!" Irritated with herself, she dismissed that sexual zing of his kiss and blamed her reaction on the steady diet of romantic dreams she'd fed herself for years. She dug out a pair of Ben's old jeans and shirt from the box marked for charity, determined to march right in there and get him out of those wet clothes before the fellow caught pneumonia. Suddenly her throat went dry at the prospect of undressing him.

Get over it, Josie. It's not like you haven't seen a naked man before.

And it wasn't, Josie reminded herself. She had been married for pity's sake. Feeling some of her calm and clearheaded self return, she armed herself with aspirin, a pitcher of water, a glass, and the clothes. She picked up her tray and headed to the bedroom to check on her patient.

A teensy measure of her newly reclaimed calm slipped when she opened the bedroom door. He lay motionless on the four-poster bed, looking too big and too male amidst the pale rose and ivory bedding. Lamplight framed his handsome face, making his hair gleam like wet gold. The white bandage on his forehead stood out in stark relief against bronzed skin. Once again the image of a golden prince came to mind.

Dismissing the fanciful thoughts, Josie made her way over to the bed. She placed the tray on the bedside table, but continued to hang on to the clothes she'd brought him. "It's time to wake up," she said. "Remember, I told you I'd have to wake you every hour? Well, it's time again. I've got some aspirin, and I've brought some dry clothes for you to change into."

Nothing. Not so much as a grunt or a flicker of an eyelid out of him.

Clearing her throat, Josie tried again, this time more forcefully. "You have to wake up now. I've brought you some aspirin to help your head and a change of clothes."

Still, nothing. He didn't move. Didn't utter a sound.

Frowning, Josie reached over and gave his shoulder a nudge. He stirred, and she snatched her hand back. "You need to take some aspirin and get out of those wet things," she said again, this time in her firmest schoolteacher's voice.

He muttered something that she suspected was no.

Annoyed now rather than nervous, his response made her more determined. It also triggered what Ben had called her do-gooder streak, and what she liked to think of as her human streak—that "something" inside her that had made her rescue a stray, or stop in the middle of a storm to help a stranger. Since she'd saved the man's life, he was her responsibility, she reasoned. Well, at least for the time being. And that meant making sure he didn't catch pneumonia. The man was going to get into dry clothes—one way or another. Besides, she thought, humor making her lips turn up at the corners. He was only a man. She hadn't managed to work as a teacher for nearly six years without learning how to exert some authority. It was the schoolteacher in her that made her put aside the clothes and sit on the bed. Slipping an arm behind his neck, she lifted him to a sitting position and with the aspirin in her palm, she tapped her finger against his lips. "Open up," she ordered.

"What the—"

She shoved the aspirin between his lips, then quickly followed with water. Strong, powerful fingers locked around her wrist at the same time that he clamped his mouth closed and sent water dribbling down the front of his already-wet shirt. The muscles in his neck had gone stiff, and his body felt like corded steel beneath her fingers. Stunned, Josie's gaze shot up to meet his. The dark eyes trained on her were just as hard as the rest of him…and wary.

"Oh, for pity's sake, it's only aspirin and water. Not poison." When he still failed to respond or release his vicelike grip on her wrist she said, "Please. You need to swallow the aspirin. I know you must be in a lot of pain with that gash on your head. The aspirin will make you feel better."

After a moment something inside him eased. His mouth lost some of the hard edge. Tipping her wrist, he drank deeply from the glass she held, but his eyes remained open, never once leaving hers. The intensity of his gaze reminded her of the wild kiss he'd given her out in the storm, and Josie felt that shivery heat spilling through her. By the time he finished the water and released her hand, she was feeling anything but calm and clearheaded. In fact, all of those female nerves were jumping inside her again.

With less-than-steady hands, she returned the glass to the tray, determined not to let him know how he had rattled her. "I'll leave you to get out of those wet things. Just yell for me if you need anything," she told him and started to leave. Then she noticed that his eyes were closed again. Frowning, she said, "Did you hear me? I'm leaving so you can change clothes."

When he still failed to respond, she jabbed a finger at his shoulder. Again, no response. "Great," she muttered. The man was obviously out cold again—either from exhaustion or from his injury or from both. Worrying at her bottom lip with her teeth, she debated what she should do. She didn't have any options, she admitted. She was going to have to get him out of his wet things and into something dry.

Josie studied her patient and frowned again. Changing the babies' clothes had been one thing. Changing their daddy's clothes was quite another. After wiping her hands on her jeans, Josie moved toward the foot of the bed. She'd start with his boots, she decided, and as she reached for the first one, she fervently wished she'd taken the dirty things off him before they'd had an opportunity to become acquainted with her comforter. *Maybe I'll be lucky and he'll wake up before I've even got the first boot off and finish the job himself.*

She wasn't lucky. He didn't wake up. The man didn't stir even after she'd made several attempts to get the blasted boots off. Finally the first one came free. Even wet, the deep brown leather was butter soft, expertly stitched and obviously expensive. From the size of the thing, she suspected he'd had them custom-made. "All right. One down. One to go," she muttered. After dropping the boot beside the bed, she reached for its mate. She gave it one hard tug, then another, and on the third tug Josie went tumbling back and onto the floor with his soggy boot in her hands and a wicked-looking gun in her lap. Stunned, Josie dropped the boot and picked up the shiny black weapon.

Oh, my heavens! What kind of man carries a gun in his boot? An escaped convict? A bank robber? A government spy?

Stop it, she told herself, and slammed the brakes on her runaway thoughts. She stared at the gun in her hands, turning the thing over, studying it. It felt hard, cold, lifeless and sent a shudder through her. Oh for pity's sake, she chided herself for her reaction. This was Texas. Half the men in the state owned a gun. Just because she didn't particularly like the things meant zip, she reasoned. Besides, hadn't she read somewhere that owning a gun was some sort of guy thing? That's probably all this was, too—a guy thing. Walking over to the armoire, she tucked the gun inside a drawer and out of sight, then turned around and went toward the bed.

Besides, discovering that the man carried a gun was the least of her problems at the moment. Getting him out of those wet clothes was. With nerves bouncing in her stomach like Ping-Pong balls, she reached for the button of his shirt.

By the time Josie had unfastened the last of his buttons and had wrestled the shirt off him, she wasn't so sure that leaving him in his wet things would have been such a bad idea after all. Although he was about the same size as her former husband had been, there the similarities ended.

While Ben had been fair-skinned, this man appeared to have been kissed by the sun. And talk about shoulders! He had linebacker shoulders, and a well-toned chest to go with them. A silver medal lay against his chest, suspended by a chain from his neck. She started to reach for the disc to examine it, then decided she'd better not. Instead she directed her attention to the other major difference between this man's body and that of her former husband's—chest hair. Ben's chest had been as smooth as a baby's bottom. But her patient had a swirl of deep gold hair that arrowed down the center of his chest all the way to the taut muscles that stretched across his abdomen and then vanished beneath the waist of his jeans. Heat curled in Josie's belly as she looked at him, struck by the masculine beauty of his body. Surprised and embarrassed by her reaction, Josie reminded herself that she had a job to do. And that job didn't include ogling the man's body and thinking inappropriate thoughts.

Inappropriate or not, by the time Josie lowered his zipper and tugged off his jeans, her fingers were shaking. And if she were being honest with herself, her accelerated breathing had little to do with exertion and everything to do with the man who lay stretched out on her bed naked—save for a pair of black briefs. Fascinated, her eyes tracked that vee of dark gold hair that disappeared beneath the low-rise briefs. And the curl of heat inside her twisted, slid lower.

Get a grip, Josie, she told herself. Or else she was going to end up embarrassing the man and making a complete fool of herself. It was the thought of making a fool of herself that snapped her back to her senses. Pride, Josie conceded, had seen her through a mountain of disappointments more times than she cared to remember. While the Almighty might have skimped on her when it came to looks and family, He had given her an abundance of pride. And it was pride that made her yank the comforter up over the man and leave the room.

He came awake as he always did—instantly and fully alert. In the blink of an eye he noted the position of the exits. Assured he was alone, and sensing no immediate danger, he gave in to the need to clutch his aching head. He didn't know what had happened, but he felt as though he'd gone ten rounds with a Mack truck. Based on the wad of gauze and tape across his forehead, he could only assume that he'd lost.

Willing himself not to focus on the pain in his head, he took quick stock of his surroundings and tried to determine where he was. He noted the ceiling painted a soft shade of cream, the delicate floral border that wrapped the room's four walls. He gazed past the empty overstuffed chair in faded chintz positioned several feet from the bed. A small dressing table covered in lace sat against the far wall, a vase of pale pink roses, glass bottles and a ceramic box sat atop it. Continuing his assessment, he skimmed past the old-fashioned armoire in one corner and paused at the quaint bench seat beneath a window decked out in mint-and-ivory-colored drapes.

Nothing about the room or its contents triggered any warning bells. Nor did the place strike any chords of familiarity. But that fact didn't alarm him. Although he had no idea

where he was or exactly how he'd gotten here, he *was* sure
of one thing—the room and the bed he occupied belonged to
a female. Pleased by the thought, he closed his eyes, drew
in a deep breath and smiled. Now *that* he did recognize—the
scent of roses and rain. And of a woman.

But who was she?

He searched his memory for a picture to match with the
scent. At first none came to him. Then an image began to
play at the fringes of his memory—an image of a raven-
haired angel with clear, green eyes leaning over him, speaking to him in a honeyed voice. The smile curving his lips
widened. Opening his eyes, he stared at the empty space in
the bed beside him and probed for a name to go with the
face of the woman whose bed he'd shared.

"Good morning."

He turned his gaze toward the doorway at the sound of the
voice and stared at its owner. "Morning," he replied, giving
her a quick once-over and then a slower one. The tray she
held blocked his view of her upper torso, but he noted with
appreciation the way the jeans hugged her long legs, the
slight sway of her hips as she walked toward the bed. His
body responded to her immediately, tightening as he thought
of her stripping off those jeans and shirt and joining him back
in bed. He started to invite her to do just that, only he
couldn't come up with her name.

"How are you feeling?"

"Fine," he replied, only to wince when a pain shot
through his head as he pushed up to his elbows. "Correction.
Not so fine. My head feels as if it went a couple of rounds
with a tank and lost."

"I'm not surprised."

He shifted to a sitting position and was surprised to discover that he still had on his briefs. Must have really tied
one on, he reasoned, which also surprised him since he
couldn't remember the last time he'd been in such sad shape.
Not only couldn't he remember her name, but he usually slept

in the raw. Heaven knows what in the devil he'd done to his
head. He was just about to ask her what had happened when
the scent of coffee derailed his thought processes. He sniffed.
"Please, tell me that's coffee I smell."

"It's coffee," she assured him with a friendly smile and
placed the tray on the table beside the bed. "After last night,
I thought you could use a cup."

After last night? Frowning he tried to remember what had
happened last night. But for the life of him, his memory of
their evening between the sheets and exactly what had led to
his monster-size headache remained blank.

"I wasn't sure if you'd be hungry or not, but I brought
some biscuits to go with the coffee just in case."

"Actually, I'm starved," he told her and realized he was.
"Biscuits sound great."

"Really? That's wonderful," she said and proceeded to
transfer biscuits to a plate.

Ah, she was eager to please, he decided and continued to
study her, contemplating her hands as she fiddled with butter
and napkins. Her nails were short, unpolished, but there was
a gracefulness in her movements. Gentle hands, soft hands,
with long soothing fingers, he thought, and another image
winked at the edges of his memory. An image of those fingers stroking his face tenderly while she spoke to him in that
lyrical voice. He lifted his gaze, noting the long column of
pale skin at her throat, the fullness of her unpainted mouth.
He tried to recall her taste, but it eluded him, just as her
name did. Disturbed that he couldn't remember kissing her,
he drew in another deep breath, and this time caught her
scent—roses and rain. Desire stirred inside him as he continued to watch her, tried to remember what it had been like to
make love to her. And once again he drew a blank. As though
sensing his scrutiny, she looked up, and her gaze tangled with
his. Suddenly the air snapped with the sexual vibrations
bouncing between them.

Just as quickly she looked away. "According to what I

read in the book I checked last night, having an appetite after an experience like this is considered a good sign.''

''Excuse me?'' She'd actually read books about what to expect from sex?

''I have to admit, you really had me worried last night,'' she said, as she handed him a napkin.

''I did?''

''Oh, yes.''

''Um, why?'' he asked, hoping for some clue.

''Well, mostly because you were so restless. You seemed to be having some disturbing dreams—which is understandable, of course.''

''Not for me, it isn't. I don't usually dream much.''

''Yes. But under these circumstances, I suspect it's only normal.''

Under these circumstances? What in the hell had happened last night?

While he desperately wanted to ask the question, he didn't. After all, how was he supposed to tell a woman whose bed he'd obviously shared that not only could he not remember making love with her, but he couldn't even remember her name? The answer was simple. He didn't tell her.

''So how do you take your coffee?''

The question gave him pause. Evidently they hadn't been lovers very long if she didn't know how he drank his coffee. ''Black, one sugar,'' he told her. Deciding he needed some answers to the questions buzzing in his head, he said, ''But the coffee can wait. There's something else I need first.''

Her fingers hovered over the sugar bowl. She tipped a glance at him. ''Oh, I'm sorry. I should have thought to ask if you wanted more aspirin for your head right off. That was a nasty cut you got. I'll just be a minute—''

''Angel,'' he said, something stirring inside him at her eagerness to please him. He reached out, captured her hand. ''I would like that aspirin—in a minute. But right now what I want is you.''

He tugged, and she squealed as she fell to the bed against him. Surprise streaked across her features when he closed his arms around her and flipped her body beneath his. "What do you think you're doing?"

She appeared so genuinely shocked and her tone so school-marm proper, he almost released her, sure he'd made a mistake. Then he caught that flicker of heat in her eyes, that shy yearning he'd glimpsed earlier when she'd looked at him, and he decided he hadn't been wrong after all. "I'm remembering," he whispered and lowered his mouth to hers.

She tasted sweet. Incredibly sweet and...innocent. And familiar. Yet not familiar at all. He nipped her bottom lip, and when she opened, he slid his tongue inside for a deeper taste. A shudder went through her, reverberated in him. When she pressed her hands against his shoulders, he lifted his head a fraction, again thinking he'd made a mistake. But one look into those soft, dreamy eyes and he knew that the only mistake about this kiss was that he didn't remember the previous ones they'd shared. So he dipped down to kiss her again and make a new set of memories for them both.

For the space of a heartbeat, she relaxed beneath him, her body molding to fit his like a glove. Her fingers curled, dug into the bare skin at his shoulders. She returned his kiss with an eagerness that surprised him, aroused him, touched some part of him that he was sure had never been touched before. Damn, how could he have forgotten her? How could he not remember this fire that they created together? One thing he was sure of, he decided, angling his head and taking the kiss deeper, he wouldn't forget making love to her this time.

So caught up in the wonder and anticipation of what was to come, several moments ticked by before he realized her fingers were no longer clinging to him, but were shoving at his chest. He lifted his head. "What's wr—"

She drew her knee up like a weapon, and he sucked in his breath at the threat. "Get off of me, you...you jerk!"

He pulled back, confused as much by her demand as by

the mixture of outrage in her voice and the panic in her eyes. "What's wrong?"

"What's wrong?" she repeated, color shooting up her pale cheeks as she scrambled off the bed. "You have the nerve to ask me that after...after mauling me?"

The accusation hit him like a sucker punch, sparking anger and sending a rush of blood through his system that made the pain in his head intensify. "Mauling?"

Another streak of color shot up her cheeks, and she looked away. "At least have the decency to cover yourself."

He looked down, noted his still-aroused state wasn't exactly hidden by the briefs. He yanked the sheet over his lower body. "All right. Now you want to tell me what's going on here? Why the mauling accusation?"

"Maybe *mauling* was a bit strong," she conceded. "But you caught me off guard. I certainly didn't expect you to kiss me."

Puzzled, he asked, "Why wouldn't I kiss you?"

Defiance gleaming in her eyes, she tipped up her chin. "Because we're strangers," she shot back.

"What in the devil are you talking about? I spent the night in your bed, didn't I?"

She gave him a wary look. "Well, yes. But I wasn't in it with you."

"You weren't?"

"Of course not. I told you, we're strangers. I never laid eyes on you before last night." She frowned. "I know everyone says not to trust strangers, but I've always gone with my instincts, and you were hardly in any shape to be a threat to me. Anyway, you needed help, and I just couldn't leave y'all out there in the storm."

Trying to make sense out of what she was saying made his head ache even more. He closed his eyes a second, massaged his temples and tried to remember. "Back up a minute, angel. You couldn't leave me out where?"

"You know where—on the side of the road where you wrecked your car."

"I was in a wreck?"

She eyed him as though he'd gone crazy. "You know you were. I don't know exactly what happened, but you wrecked your car."

Panic started to sneak its way into his blood as he tried to remember driving through a storm, having an accident. He drew another blank. So he tried something simple—what day it was, where he was. When he came up empty again, he told himself to remain calm. He touched the bandage on his forehead. "I hit my head in the accident."

"Yes. At least I think that's what happened. There was a lot of blood, and you've got a really nasty cut. You should have gone to the hospital. But the storm was awful, and I was afraid I wouldn't make it back to town, so I brought you here instead."

Which explained the headache and his fuzzy memories. "And exactly where is here?"

"My farm."

"Thank you for stopping to help me."

She nodded. "You still need to see a doctor, and I'm pretty sure that cut needs to be stitched. But the rain's still coming down. The road's under water now, and the phone lines have been out since last night, so I haven't been able to notify the sheriff about the accident."

"It's no big deal, and I'm sure my head will be fine," he told her, instinctively shying away from the thought of her calling hospitals or the law.

"The worst part is that without the phone, there's no way for you to even notify your wife that y'all are okay."

"My what?" he said, jerking his attention back to her and sending pain slicing through his skull at the quick movement.

"Your wife," she repeated.

"Angel, I don't have a wife," he informed her, then realized he couldn't remember if he had a wife or not. At least he didn't think he had one. For some reason the thought of being married had acid churning in his stomach. He darted a glance at her hands and was relieved to see no jewelry at all.

"I see," she said, censure in her voice.

"I'm certainly glad one of us does," he muttered, puzzled by her disapproval.

"Pardon?"

He sighed. "I, um, I'm having a bit of trouble remembering certain things."

"Like what?"

"Like last night. Did you and I— Did we—?"

"No," she said, her cheeks pinkening. "I slept on the couch."

"Sorry." And he was. Judging by the sparks they generated, he suspected the two of them would be good together in bed. He couldn't help noting the way she kept crumpling and then smoothing out the napkin that she'd picked up from the floor. Nerves, he decided, and for some reason found her flustered state endearing. Maybe they would be lovers yet, he mused. That is, as soon as he started remembering things. "I appreciate everything you've done. But there's one other thing I'd like to ask you to do for me, if you would."

"Yes?"

"Tell me your name."

"Josie," she told him. "Josie Walters."

"Josie," he repeated the name, trying out the sound of it on his lips and deciding he liked it. "Am I correct in assuming there's no Mr. Walters?"

"I'm a widow. My husband died about a year ago."

"Sorry for your loss, and for the misunderstanding."

"No problem," she said, giving him a shy smile. "But you never did tell me what your name is."

Extending his hand, he said, "I'm... I'm..." Panic began to churn in his blood again, making his head throb. Sweat broke out across his brow. He tried not to give in to that panic as he groped for some memory, any memory, of what his name was, who he was, where he was from. But try as he might, his memory was an empty page that began and ended with Josie's face, the sound of her voice.

"What is it? What's wrong?"

"I don't have any idea who I am."

Three

"What do you mean, you don't know who you are?"

"Just what I said." Stripping off the covers, he sat up on the side of the bed, shoved his hands through his hair. "I can't remember who I am."

The despair in his voice touched something deep inside Josie. So did the sight of his near-naked body. Despite her marriage, she'd had little experience when it came to men. Certainly not with gorgeous men who seemed inclined to kiss her. Averting her gaze from all that bronzed skin and muscle, she insisted, "But you must remember *something*."

He pinned her with eyes that had gone flat and hard. "I don't remember a damn thing—except for you."

"Me?" The word came out as little more than a squeak. She swallowed, tried again. "But that doesn't make any sense. Why would you remember me? We don't even know each other."

He shrugged. "Doesn't matter. And it doesn't change the fact that I can't remember my name. I certainly don't remember any accident or hitting my head.'' He rubbed at his temple as though in pain, but when he lifted those chocolate eyes to hers, they were filled with irritation…and with need.

Josie's stomach tightened like a fist.

"The only thing that I do remember is *you*. Your face. The sound of your voice. Even the way you smell. When you came walking through that door a few minutes ago, I could have sworn that you and I were—"

"Um, yes. I, um, get the picture," Josie told him. And she did. She knew exactly what he'd thought, given the way he'd tumbled her to the bed and kissed her. Even now just thinking about that kiss made her knees sag. And considering the way she'd responded, was it any wonder the man had thought they were lovers?

How could she have behaved that way? Allowed him such liberties? Taken such liberties herself? Her behavior had been outrageous. She'd obviously taken temporary leave of her senses. What else could account for that heady sensation she'd experienced? Or the fact that she'd actually enjoyed being wrapped in his arms, of feeling his hard body pressed against hers, of discovering the taste and texture of his mouth? And that mouth! She hadn't known a mouth could be so skilled, so hungry, so eager. Not for her.

Her lips tingled at the memory, and she pressed her fingertips against them. No one had ever kissed her that way before. Not even in the early days of her marriage had she experienced that kind of passion—so powerful, so huge, so consuming. During those few moments desire had exploded inside her, obliterating her ability to think. Even now, just remembering sent shivers of longing curling through her— confusing her, shaming her and exciting her all at the same time. For a woman who had always considered herself less than hot natured when it came to sex, and had even accepted that she was at least partly responsible for Ben's straying, her response to this stranger's kiss made absolutely no sense. Yet there was no denying that she'd wanted more. What did that say about her character? Not much, she decided. Squeezing her eyes shut, she could only be grateful that he hadn't realized just how close to the edge she had been. That one kiss from him had had her swimming in those fairy-tale dreams again.

"Damn it! Why can't I remember anything?"

Josie's eyes snapped open at the sharpness in his tone, saw him wince and grab his head. "You've got to calm down," she told him. "Getting upset isn't going to help matters. That blow to your head must have caused some sort of temporary amnesia."

He fingered the bandage on his forehead, traced the square of white gauze and tape. "Amnesia," he repeated with a frown, then lifted his eyes to hers. "How long does that usually last?"

"I...um...I'm not sure," Josie admitted.

"Well, how long do you think? A day? Two days? A week?"

"It isn't the flu," she informed him, irritated by his impatience. "From the few things I remember reading about amnesia, each case varies. Some people get their memory back in a few days. Some take weeks or months, even years. And others, well, others take...longer."

Something in her tone must have alarmed him because he narrowed his eyes. "How much longer?"

"Some people never get their memory back."

"I'll get mine back," he assured her with a steel in his voice that matched the determination in his eyes.

"I'm sure you will." At least she hoped he would. "But in the meantime, you need to rest."

"I don't want to rest. I want to find out who I am," he said, frustration emanating from him in waves. The fingers rubbing at his temples stopped abruptly, and he whipped his attention to her. "What about ID? I must have had some sort of identification on me. A driver's license? Credit cards?"

She shook her head. "I'm sorry. All I found was a money

clip with the initial *B* and a wad of bills. If you had a wallet, I guess it's possible it's still in the car. I didn't take the time to look too closely. Or it could have fallen on the road when you got out of your car.'' And if that were the case, they would never find it, thanks to the rising water and wind, she added silently. ''When the storm lets up, I'll drive out to where you had the wreck and see what I can find.''

''No. I'll go. It's my problem, and I've already put you to enough trouble.''

She shrugged, seeing no point in arguing that he really wasn't well and shouldn't be behind the wheel of any vehicle. ''Well, neither one of us will be going anywhere until this storm lets up.'' She paused, wondering whether she should tell him what else she had found.

He turned laser-sharp eyes on her. ''What is it? What aren't you telling me?''

It unnerved her that he could read her so clearly, and made her pray he hadn't been able to read how attracted she was to him. ''Besides the money clip and cash, you had a gun. It was hidden in one of your boots.''

The frown creasing his brow deepened, but he said nothing, simply continued to watch her.

''I put it over there, in the top drawer.'' She pointed to the armoire in the corner. ''The money clip and cash are with it.''

Still silent, he pushed to his feet. And when he swayed, she reached out instinctively to steady him, and another sizzle of heat rippled through her. Awareness, lightning quick, flashed into his eyes. He sank back down to the bed, and Josie snatched her hand away. ''Guess my head's not as hard as I thought. The damned…darned thing feels like somebody took a hammer to it,'' he muttered.

''I'll go, and let you get some rest.''

''No,'' he responded quickly. ''I've had enough rest. I'd like to get dressed and then take a look at that money clip and gun. Maybe seeing them will trigger my memory.'' He stood again, this time steady.

Unable to stop herself, Josie stared at him. He had a magnificent body. Tall, strong, solid. He reminded her of a mythical god, a warrior prince cast in bronze and gold, she thought. She ran her gaze over him and paused at a jagged scar on one shoulder, wondering how he'd gotten it. She skimmed past the flat stomach, and shifted lower to where his sex strained against the black briefs. Liquid heat spilled through her as she recalled the feel of him pressed hot and heavy against her thighs. Recognizing the dangerous direction of her thoughts, Josie forced her gaze up to his face. But looking into his eyes proved no safer. They were dark, mysterious and burned with a sensual fire that had the air backing up in her lungs.

''Angel, unless you've changed your mind about joining me in this bed, I think you'd better stop looking at me like that and let me get dressed.''

Mortified to have been caught gawking at him like a love-struck schoolgirl, she took a step back to allow him to pass.

But he made no attempt to leave. Instead he stood there looking impossibly sexy and tempting. The bandage on his forehead added an edge of danger to his appeal, but was at odds with the hint of a smile on his lips.

''Is there a problem?'' she asked, irritated and hurt that he found the mousy little widow's fascination with him funny.

''No. I just realized that you must have been the one to undress me last night.''

Her pride pricked that she'd made herself such a vulnerable target by gaping at him. She hiked up her chin. ''It was either that or let you catch pneumonia. You were soaked to the skin.''

''Hey, I wasn't complaining. At least not about you undressing me. I just think it's a shame that I don't remember.'' The grin he flashed her was quick, reckless and did strange things to her pulse.

"Nothing to remember except being wet and cold," she informed him primly. Feigning a nonchalance she was far from feeling, Josie said, "You might want to put on some clothes."

"Be happy to. But first you'll need to tell me where I can find them."

Color stained her cheeks, and she once again wanted to cringe over letting the man rattle her so badly. "Your things are in the bathroom. I hung them there to dry last night. I'll get them," she offered, eager to put some distance between them.

"That's all right," he told her, catching her by the arm as she started to turn away. Another stab of heat shot through Josie at his touch, making her heart slap against her ribs to the beat of a Texas two-step. From the expression on his face, she wasn't the only one having trouble breathing. "I'll get them," he said, his voice rough, gravelly. "I need to use the facilities, anyway."

Sure she'd swallow her tongue if she tried to respond, Josie simply nodded. And not until the bathroom door closed behind him was she able to breathe again. *Get a grip, Josie. Now is not the time to be hit with your very first lust attack! You've got to think, girl. Think!*

But thinking around him wasn't an easy task, she admitted, as she walked over to the window and sank down to the floral cushion that covered the bench seat. She stared out into the storm that continued to rage outside. A perfect reflection of her own feelings, she mused. None of it made any sense— not her reaction to his man or the predicament she found herself in.

And she *was* in a predicament. A real fix, Sister Mary Claire would have called it. She was all alone, isolated on a remote farm nearly two hours from the nearest town with a sexy stranger who claimed to have no memory, but who rattled her common sense and awakened hormones in her that she hadn't even known she'd possessed. To make matters worse, the normally dry creek bed that ran alongside the road leading to her farm had already overflowed when she'd checked earlier this morning—which meant driving him into Royal or Midland or asking the sheriff from either town to come out here to get him was not an option. Of course, added to the list was the problem of the babies.

The babies! For Pete's sake! She smacked her forehead. She hadn't even told him about the babies. Surely seeing his children would help him remember who he was.

And remind him that he had a wife?

The question sneaked itself right into her thoughts. Despite his claim that he wasn't married and the fact that he lacked a wedding band, she knew darn well the man hadn't come by those two little darlings by himself. Having been on the receiving end of a cheating husband herself, she certainly didn't want to be the cause of some other woman's pain. Because whoever the woman was—wife or girlfriend—she had helped him create two adorable children.

A tender ache blossomed inside Josie as she thought about the twins. What would it be like to be their mother? To hold their little mouths to her breast as she nursed them, to cradle them in her arms and love them? She had been so sure she would have a houseful of babies of her own by now.

But no babies had grown inside her. Not a single one. She pressed her hand to her flat belly. Ben had claimed he wasn't ready to be a father, had wanted to wait. Even if he hadn't died, she wasn't sure there would have ever been any babies—given the troubles in their marriage. But, oh, how she'd wanted a child of her own, someone to give all the love she had stored up in her heart. Josie brought the heel of her hand to her chest, rubbed at the spot where her heart beat.

She heard the door to the bathroom open, and Josie shoved her sad thoughts aside as he came walking into the bedroom again—this time wearing jeans and with a towel draped around his neck. Lord, but the man was beautiful.

"I found an unopened toothbrush in the medicine cabinet and used it. I hope you don't mind."

"Of course not." She slid off the bench seat and started toward him, intent on telling him about the babies. "I don't know what's the matter with me. How I could have forgotten to tell you—"

One of the babies started to cry, flooding the quiet house with an unhappy wail.

"What the—" He jerked his gaze toward the doorway, then back to her. "What was that?"

"A baby. That's what I started to tell you. You—"

"You have a kid?"

"Me? That's not my—"

The second baby got in on the act and started to cry with its twin, creating a set of sobs that would break any mother's heart or make her tone-deaf if she wasn't careful.

He groaned, held a hand to his head and looked back at her. "Jeez. How many kids do you have, anyway?"

"I don't have any." She winced as the cries reached an all-time high note that Josie thought would shatter glass. She made a dash for the door. "But you have two...twins."

Her reply hit him like a prizefighter's punch, paralyzing him for long seconds. Speechless, he watched Josie's cute little tush clear the room, her long legs moving at a fast clip. Unable to move, after the bomb she'd dropped on him, he stood there with his mouth open, his bare feet planted on the floor, his head spinning. The room swam before him. Damn near sure he was going to pass out, he braced his hands against the wall and sucked in air. The dizziness subsided, leaving him feeling as weak as a kitten and wishing he could just start the entire day over. And he'd start it by remembering who he was and erasing that little bombshell Josie had just dropped on him.

But wishing wasn't worth spit. Wishing couldn't solve his problems. Only he could. And he intended to do just that—

starting with Josie. Shoving away from the wall, he moved toward the door on legs not quite as steady as he'd like them to be. What he wouldn't give to just sit down—preferably with a shot of good Irish whisky, he mused. And he would. Just as soon as he set a certain raven-haired woman straight about a major misconception on her part. All right. Maybe he had lost his memory, and he didn't remember his name. But he was damn sure about one thing—he was *not* anyone's daddy.

Daddy!

Just the idea made him shudder. Him? A father? No way! The very notion was absurd. Just the thought of being responsible for one baby, let alone two, sent fear crawling down his spine. Surely this was not the reaction of a man who had kids. Besides, loss of memory or not, what he knew about kids wouldn't fill a nutshell. If he were a father—which he didn't believe for a minute that he was—he sure as hell would have remembered the fact.

Wouldn't he? A man just didn't forget that sort of thing, he reasoned. Nope. He wasn't any squalling, pint-size person's daddy. To even think he was had been a mistake. And Miss Josie Walters with the angel eyes and sulky mouth had been the one to make it. Intent on telling her just that, he started down the hall to find her.

Finding Josie proved easy enough. He simply followed the sound of the lullaby she was singing. He paused in the doorway of the kitchen. For some, it would be an appealing picture, he thought, watching her sway with the baby in her arms as she sang. He shifted his focus from Josie and the baby to the white pine table, barely visible beneath the matching baby seats. Some instinct had him quickly scope out the rest of the room and note the points of exit—a door armed with a set of brass locks and a pair of large windows over a double sink. Crisp white curtains with yellow and blue flowers framed the window and were tied at either side, allowing a view of gray skies and steady rain. But he dismissed the weather conditions to study the window's dimensions. He frowned, noting that the space was large enough for a man to crawl through it. Of course, the man would have to get past the jungle of plants and flowers that Josie had cluttering the sill first. Satisfied that was unlikely to happen without alerting him, he averted his gaze to the stove where a pot of something that smelled delicious simmered. Pressing a hand to his grumbling stomach, he wondered how long it had been since he'd last eaten.

Putting thoughts of food on hold, he continued his assessment of the room. A side-by-side refrigerator and dishwasher, both in white, crowded one wall. An old-fashioned breakfront took up the major part of another. Atop it, a fistful of yellow roses spilled from a sapphire-colored bottle. Pine cabinets fitted with glass doors and little white knobs filled another wall. A long sweep of white counter stretched beneath the cabinets and more pine cabinets filled the space below the counter. And everywhere he looked there were framed needlework samplers, knickknacks, homey touches. What little of the wall remained bare had been painted a cheery shade of lemon.

The room was crowded, bordered on outright clutter, he concluded. Yet it struck him as warm and welcoming. So did the woman at its center. She stood in profile, those lean hips of hers swaying slowly while she crooned a dreamy lullaby to the baby in her arms. He shouldn't have found the picture arousing.

But he did.

He shouldn't have recalled so clearly the taste of her mouth.

But he did.

And he certainly shouldn't have itched to move behind her, to slide his hands beneath her flannel shirt and discover if her skin was as soft and warm as he imagined.

Yet he did.

There was something so basically female, so innocent and

at the same time so overtly sensual, about the way she cradled the baby to her breast while she sang. Somehow she managed to look wholesome and sexy at the same time. The combination was staggering.

Suddenly, as though some sixth sense alerted her that she was no longer alone, Josie stopped singing midnote and whirled around to face him. "Goodness! You gave me a scare," she said, her voice a breathless whisper that had his body tightening with need. "I didn't hear you come in here."

"Sorry. I didn't mean to scare you."

"I'm not usually so jumpy. Must be this weather," she offered with a half-hearted smile.

The weather or him? he wondered, at the look in her eyes. Lord, but she really did have incredible eyes—a clear green, with a rim of black circling the iris. They were eyes a man could easily find himself lost in if he wasn't careful. He covered the distance between them, aware of the coolness of the wood floor beneath his bare feet, at odds with the heat stirring in his loins. He was sure she wasn't even aware of it and would probably be mortified if she knew that he recognized the way her eyes assessed his body appreciatively. When her gaze returned to his face, another quick jolt of desire fired through him at the shy yearning in her eyes. What would it be like to see Josie's eyes cloud with desire? To watch that soft green go nearly black with anticipation as he filled her?

No way did he intend to find out, he told himself, yanking his gaze and his thoughts in another direction. Something told him Josie Walters was not the sort of woman to hop into the sack with a man without her emotions being involved. Memory or not, the idea of emotional tangles made him edgy. One more reason he was sure he couldn't be those kids' dad.

"Okay, sweetie. How about a little burp for Aunt Josie?". she murmured to the baby she held. Removing the bottle from its puckered mouth, she shifted the baby to her shoulder and started to pat its back. She flicked a glance at him. "I didn't think to ask you. Did you want to burp him?"

"When you burp the baby, be sure to support its back."

His throat went desert dry as the instructions popped into his head, whispered by some faceless female voice. "Uh, no thanks."

"You sure? Holding your...holding him might trigger your memory."

Panic began to knot in his stomach. "I don't think so. I told you. I'm not their father. Besides, it looks to me like you know what you're doing." He paused. "You do, don't you? I mean taking care of babies is one of those womanly instinct things, right?"

"Hardly," she said, disdain in her voice. "But I do know the basics. Most of the foster homes I lived in when I was growing up had babies in them. I used to help out when I wasn't in school. But that's not to say I'm any expert. I mean, I've never..." She paused, swallowed. "I've never had any babies of my own."

But she'd wanted to, he guessed, by the catch in her voice. "Well, you definitely know more than me."

Her lips thinned in disapproval. "How can you say that when you have these two beautiful babies? Just because you have amnesia—"

"Listen, I know you think I'm their father because they were with me. But I'm telling you, I can't be."

"Why not?"

"Well, because I may not remember anything else, but I'd surely remember my own kids."

"What makes you think that? You said yourself, you don't remember your own name."

"That's different."

"How?" she argued.

"It just is."

"Then how do you explain them being with you?"

"I can't," he admitted. Frustrated, he offered, "Maybe I was baby-sitting them for a friend or for a relative."

She cocked one eyebrow, gave him a considering look.

"No offense. But you don't exactly strike me as the baby-sitter type."

He agreed. "Yeah, well, it's the best I can come up with under the circumstances. I just know in my gut that these guys are not mine."

The baby let out a loud burp, ending the discussion. "Good boy," Josie said with a smile as she eased him into the crook of her arm. She picked up the bottle and brought it to his mouth. The little guy latched on to it greedily.

"He's a boy, then?" he asked, aware of the baby watching him out of big blue eyes.

"Umm-hmm. This is Edward. That little heartbreaker over there is his twin sister Miranda."

Edward? Miranda? His gaze ping-ponged from Josie and the infant in her arms to the baby whimpering in the carrier on the table, then back to Josie again. "How do you know their names? I thought—"

A wail from Miranda cut him off.

Josie was beside the other infant in a flash. "Shh. It's okay, sweetie," Josie soothed, stroking the little cheek. She slipped a pacifier between the baby's lips. "They were both wearing ID bracelets with those names engraved on them."

His eyes and Josie's immediately darted to his left wrist. He ripped off the gold and steel watch, searched the band for a name. Nothing. The thing was obviously expensive, but it bore nothing beyond the pricy brand name and the stamp declaring the gold to be fourteen karats. Disappointed, he looked up into Josie's expectant face and shook his head.

"What about the babies? Do their names ring any bells?"

He thought for a moment, searched for some flicker of recognition. "No," he admitted. As though she was unhappy with his answer, Miranda began to cry again—this time harder—and her cries set off her twin.

Still holding Edward in her arms, Josie turned to the crying baby. She stroked the little wet cheek, brushed tufts of blond hair with her fingers. "It's all right, love. Aunt Josie will feed you just as soon as your brother's finished," she promised and slipped the pacifier into the infant's mouth again.

The baby promptly spit it out again, and it landed at Blake's feet. He scooped the thing up, rinsed it off as he'd seen Josie do. But when he tried to offer the nipple to the baby, she cried even harder and held out her little arms to him. "What's wrong with it?" he asked, pointing to the little red-faced noisemaker sporting a pink ribbon.

"Her," Josie corrected. "She's either hungry, wet, wants to be held or all three." Propping the other baby up on her shoulder, she took the pacifier and offered it to the screaming Miranda again.

Once more she spit the thing out and continued to cry. Josie shot him a look. "Listen, you're going to have to help me here."

"Me?" He took a step back, nerves jumping at the prospect. "I told you, they're not mine."

"They're not mine, either," she informed him, a determined gleam in her eye.

"I don't know anything about babies," he argued.

"Then it's time you learned. Come on, it's not that difficult."

"Speak for yourself."

When her eyes narrowed and she hiked up her chin militantly, he knew the battle was over. Swallowing, he told himself he could do this. Babies were just miniature people, right? Right, he answered silently. How difficult could it be to handle a minisize person? "Okay, what do I do?"

"Try giving her the bottle. It's over there on the counter."

But when he retrieved the thing and offered it to the sobbing infant, she pushed it away. She held out those tiny arms to him and continued to wail. When the other baby started whimpering, his head started to ache again. "I think it, um, she's sick or something. She doesn't want the bottle." At just that moment, the little red-faced monster let loose with an ear-shattering squeal that made him groan. "Jeez. Can't you make her stop that?"

The look she shot him could have withered iron, he decided. Jostling the still-whimpering Edward to her other shoulder, she told him, "No, I can't stop her from crying. As you can see, I've got my hands full with Edward. You'll need to check her and see if she needs her diaper changed."

When he hesitated, she pinned him with eyes that had gone as cool as a Minnesota winter. He reached over, peeled back the edge of the baby's diaper and snuck a peak. "Looks okay."

"Stick your fingers in and feel," she commanded.

Reluctantly he patted the padded fabric quickly and nearly sighed with relief. "Dry," he said unable to keep back a grin.

"Well, if she's not hungry and she doesn't need changing, she evidently wants to be held. You're going to have to pick her up, pal."

"But—"

"No buts," she countered, with the swiftness and authority of a Marine sergeant. "If you think you dislike hearing her cry, just wait. These two feed off of each other's moods. As long as one of them is crying, the other one will cry, too. Believe me, you don't want this little guy to really get started. Because if he does, it's going to get a lot worse."

And because he didn't think he could endure that racket in stereo, he wiped his hands on the towel still hanging around his neck and reached for the baby. Feeling awkward and as though his hands were too big to hold something this little, he lifted the squalling baby from her seat and held her against his shoulder, bracing her back with his hand the way he'd seen Josie do with the other baby. To his surprise the tears stopped almost at once. She gave one hiccupping sob, then another, before burying her little tear-dampened face against his neck.

And damn if something inside him didn't just melt. Overwhelmed by the unfamiliar tenderness running through him, he slanted Josie a glance. "What do I do now?" he all but whispered.

The smile she gave him made his heart pick up a beat. "Just keep doing what you're doing. When she settles a little more, see if she'll take her bottle."

A few minutes later he shifted the baby into his arms and stared down at the chubby-cheeked face. Taking the bottle Josie handed him, he brought it to the little rosebud mouth. She opened and began to suck, but those tear-filled blue eyes remained trained on his face while her fat baby fingers reached up to pat his jaw. When those fingers hooked his bottom lip and pulled, another crack started around his heart. He looked over at Josie, found her eyes on him. "Don't get any ideas," he told her, sure he knew from the expression on her face what she was thinking. "I am not her father."

"How do you know? How can you be so sure?"

"I just am," he tossed back.

"Listen, I realize this is a lot to take in, but think about it. Nothing else makes any sense. These two can't be more than four or five months old—not exactly ideal traveling companions. If you're not their father, what other reason would they have been with you in the first place?"

"I don't know," he said, frustrated because he didn't have the answer. The truth was, holding the baby did seem familiar, yet at the same time not familiar, which not only confused him, but scared the pants off him. There was something, some sense of urgency, that played at the edges of his memory, just out of reach. Try as he might, he just couldn't seem to grasp it. "I can't explain it. I just know they aren't mine."

"Well, I certainly wish they were mine," Josie said as she stared at the dozing baby in her arms.

He caught the wistfulness in her voice, saw the yearning on her face as she cradled the infant. He could easily imagine her holding a miniature Josie—a baby with green eyes and pitch-black hair. "If you ask me, these two look as if they could pass for yours."

"Mine?"

"Sure. They've both got pale skin like yours. And this little lady has a small turned-up nose just like yours."

She smiled at that. "Their skin's pale because they're new. You did notice that I have black hair and that these two are blondes, didn't you?"

"I noticed," he informed her, taking in the wisps of hair that had managed to escape her braid.

"And did you also notice that you're dark blond?"

He shrugged, ran a finger over the pale, silky curls tied with a strip of pink ribbon on top of the baby's head. Realizing what he was doing, he quickly withdrew his hand. "Yeah, but my eyes are brown, and this little gal's are blue."

Josie chuckled. "Most babies have blue eyes when they're born. Sometimes it takes as much as a year before they change color. Of course, it's possible Miranda and Edward's mother has blue eyes and theirs won't change."

Their mother. He wondered about the woman. Who was she? And why had she entrusted her children to him? Once more the answers evaded him. Propping Miranda against his shoulder, he attempted to burp her while Josie went to put the sleeping Edward to bed. Deep in thought, he paced the kitchen floor and struggled to remember as he patted the baby's back. When he heard her burp, he grinned and eased her head from his shoulder. "Good going, sugar britches," he said and watched the little mouth curve into what he hoped was a smile and not gas. Her little fingers reached out, grabbed at his nose this time. After a few tugs and twists, she decided to take off his ear.

"You two having fun?"

Laughing, he cut a glance to the doorway and drank in the sight of Josie. More of that pitch-black hair of hers had escaped from the thick braid she wore down her back and framed her narrow face, softening it, playing up her cheekbones and the wide mouth. Her skin was pale, the color of fresh cream, and he suspected the flush staining her cheeks was due to his scrutiny and not to cosmetics. From the way she continued to trap her bottom lip with her teeth, he suspected she was nervous again. And that once again he was the cause. Not that he blamed her. If she had any idea how much he would like to taste that mouth of hers, taste her again, she'd probably kick his butt out in the rain and bolt the door behind him. Forcing himself to rein in his thoughts, he said, "I'd say sugar britches here is the one having all the fun. She's tried to take off my nose, twist off my ear and right now I think she plans to eat my neck."

Josie laughed. "Want me to take her? I think it'd be best if we kept them on the same nap schedule."

"She's all yours," he told her. But when he started to hand Miranda over, something tugged at his neck. "Hey, short stuff. What've you got there?"

Josie stepped closer. "It's the medal," she informed him.

Then he noted Miranda's little mouth fastened around a disc he wore suspended from a chain around his neck. Hope sluiced through his veins as he disengaged the baby from her treasure. "Sugar britches, you're beautiful," he told her. After kissing the top of her head, he handed Miranda off to Josie.

"I forgot about the medal," Josie told him. Her eyes darted to his and back to the medal as he removed the chain from his neck. "I saw it last night when I put you to bed and meant to check it, but got busy with the babies. I was going to check it out this morning."

But she hadn't had the chance to, he realized, because he'd distracted her when he'd tumbled her to the bed and kissed her. At the time, his identity had been the last thing on his mind. Whipping the towel from his shoulders, he wiped off the baby drool and stared at the silver disc of a knight fighting a dragon. "Strange medal," he muttered.

"It's Saint George. He's the patron saint of soldiers," she

told him. At the arch in his brow, she explained, "I spent most of my childhood in a Catholic orphanage. You get to know a lot about the saints. Turn it over. See if there's any inscription."

There was.

He heard Josie's gasp even before he read the words.

"Blake— Take care while slaying those dragons. Love, Lily."

Four

"**B**lake." He repeated the name as though trying it on for size.

There was no reason to feel disappointed, Josie reasoned. She'd known from the first that there was most likely a woman in his life. Probably even a wife. The man had twins, for pity's sake! And wedding ring or not, men like this one did not lack for female company. That she'd allowed herself, for even a moment, to think otherwise had been beyond foolish. It had been just plain dumb. Just as dumb as all those fairy-tale dreams that had been a part of her daily diet for far too long. Well, she'd sworn off those silly dreams, hadn't she? And she could just swear off any romantic notions she might have had about him. She'd simply add handsome strangers with chocolate eyes and steamy kisses to the list of impossible dreams.

"Sugar britches, I love you."

Startled from her musings, Josie barely had time to register what he'd said before he leaned close to her and planted a

noisy kiss on baby Miranda's head, then swept them both
into his arms. Josie gasped as he spun them around in a
circle. "What are you doing?"

"Celebrating," he informed her, and executed another
spin.

"Blake! Put me down," she ordered, but couldn't manage
any heat behind the words—not when both he and the baby
seemed to be enjoying themselves so much. Instead, she
found herself laughing along with him.

"Can you believe it, angel? Can you believe that little
sugar britches here found out my name for me? I'm Blake.
My name is Blake," he informed her, a silly grin lighting up
his face. He planted another kiss on Miranda's tiny head,
which earned him a toothless smile, then gave her a quick
smack on the lips, too.

Josie struggled to catch her breath, to slow the quickened
beat of her heart. Emotions jumbled inside her as he lowered
her so that her feet touched the floor again. "Blake, does that
mean—"

He captured her face in his hands. And as he moved in
with his mouth, she forgot what she'd been planning to ask
him. Bracing herself for the jolt, she closed her eyes and
waited for his lips to touch hers. The jolt hit at the first brush
of his lips, an electric spark that short-circuited her system
and made her body turn to liquid. But when she would have
stepped back, given her body and heart a chance to recover,
he continued to hold her face in his hands, continued to move
that skilled mouth of his across hers lazily, seductively,
temptingly. That first jolt spun into a hum, and the hum gave
way to a slow sizzle in her blood. Then Josie forgot all about
the vices she'd just sworn off, including this man. She forgot
all about thinking and common sense. She forgot all about
what a fool she was making of herself and the heartache she
would be letting herself in for if she didn't nip this attraction
now. She forgot about everything—except for the feel of
Blake's mouth caressing her mouth, the feel of his teeth

gently nibbling at her lips, the feel of his tongue stroking the spot where he'd bitten, the joy of having him slip his tongue inside to taste her. So lost was she in his kiss that it took several seconds before she registered that the squirming sensation against her chest wasn't her heart straining to be free. It was the baby.

Mortified, Josie yanked her mouth free. She stepped back, her legs faltering a second as her knees sagged. Still clutching Miranda, she worked to slow her galloping pulse. When she finally lifted her gaze to his, the raw desire she saw there set her pulse racing all over again.

He took a step toward her.

She retreated. "Don't."

"But…"

"I need to be able to think, and I can't think when you kiss me."

Grinning, he reached for her.

"I mean it. Back off." Giving herself a mental shake, she finally focused on what she'd been planning to ask him. "Is your memory starting to come back now?"

The smile slipped from his lips. "Not exactly."

His response confused her, concerned her. "But when you said that your name was Blake. I thought…I assumed the medal triggered your memory. That you remembered that you were the Blake in the inscription."

"I *am* the Blake in the inscription. Or at least I'm pretty sure that I'm him." He sighed, shoved a hand through his hair.

"You're pretty sure?"

"The name feels 'right.' And since I am wearing the medal," he continued, closing his fingers around the disc that hung from his neck, "it stands to reason that I'm the Blake this refers to."

Her legs even less steady now than when he'd kissed her, Josie sank to one of the chairs at the kitchen table. "Then you still don't remember."

He shook his head. "Everything's mostly blank."

At Miranda's whimpers, Josie dragged her attention from the man standing shirtless before her, looking far too dangerous for her peace of mind. She shifted the baby in her arms and picked up the bottle to feed her. Striving to keep her voice neutral, Josie asked, "What about the name Lily? Do you remember if she's—" Her throat suddenly dry, she licked her lips and decided to rephrase the question. "Do you have any idea who she is?"

"Not a clue. The name doesn't ring any bells." He began to pace the length of the small kitchen like a jungle cat. A sleek, beautiful panther, she decided, noting the way the black jeans fitted across his butt, how the sun-darkened muscles in his shoulders and back rippled as he moved. When he turned around and faced her again, his eyes had gone nearly black. "But whoever Lily is, she isn't my wife."

"How do you know?" Josie asked, proud at how normal she was able to sound. Removing the bottle from Miranda's mouth, she shifted the baby to her shoulder to burp her.

"Because I know."

She stared at that unsmiling mouth. Dangerous, she told herself, and forced her gaze back up to his. "But how can you know when you can't remember?"

"The same way I know that the twins aren't mine. Because I know it here," he told her, angling a thumb at his middle. "I can feel it. Whoever this Lily is, she is not my wife."

Foolish or not, she wanted to believe him. And because she wanted to, Josie scooted away from the table, away from those piercing dark eyes and the temptation he represented. She jostled the baby, patting Miranda's diaper-clad bottom. "All right. Maybe you're right. Maybe this Lily isn't your wife."

"She isn't."

"It still doesn't tell us who you are beyond the name Blake. Since we can't go back to your car to search for an ID until the weather clears, maybe you should concentrate

on the medal. Does the line about slaying dragons mean any
thing to you?''

Blake frowned as he fingered the medal, creating a sharp
line across his forehead that disappeared beneath the ban
dage. ''No,'' he said disgustedly.

Suddenly an idea struck her. ''Blake, you were carrying a
gun and wearing a medal of St. George. St. George is the
patron saint of soldiers. Maybe you're in the military,'' she
offered.

''I guess it's possible,'' he said as though chewing over
the idea. He looked down at his jeans. ''Obviously, if I am,
I wasn't in uniform. Do you remember seeing any kind of
military uniform in the car? Maybe a jacket or a hat lying on
the seat?''

Josie thought back to the quick visual sweep she'd given
the interior of the car. ''No,'' she admitted. ''The twins' jack
ets were that camouflage pattern, but I thought it was a fash
ion thing. Not military.''

''Anything else?''

''No.''

She rocked Miranda in her arms, noted the flutter of lashes
against the baby-soft cheeks. Grateful the baby was finally
drifting off, she deliberately kept her voice low as she said,
''After I got the twins and you into my truck, I went back
for the diaper bags and then headed here. I didn't see any
other bags or things inside the car—not even a flight bag or
anything for you. Just the baby stuff. But it doesn't mean
there wasn't something in the trunk. To be honest, it didn't
even occur to me to check. The babies were crying. You were
bleeding, and the storm seemed to be getting worse by the
minute.'' If she had taken another moment to check the trunk,
would they both have been spared this not knowing who he
was? Would she still be agonizing over who the mysterious
Lily was?

''Hey, you did the smart thing. You got me and the twins

out of there. As far as your stopping to help us, it was a very brave and foolish thing to do.''

''But, I—''

He held up a hand to stem her protest, then cupped her cheek. ''It was very brave and very foolish. And I'm grateful that you did, Josie. I owe you my life, and those two munchkins' lives, too.''

''I did what anyone would have done,'' she countered, turning away from the warmth of his touch.

''Not everyone.'' He dropped his hand, looked at the baby she held and smoothed a finger along the tiny cheek. ''Because of me, she and her brother could have been killed. When I think what might have happened to them if you hadn't come along—''

''Don't,'' Josie said, a fist tightening around her heart at the idea of any harm coming to the twins. A shudder went through her as she recalled discovering that very morning that the always-dry creek bed had overflowed during the night—which meant the road where she'd found Blake and the twins was now under water. She didn't even want to think about what might have happened had she not come along when she had.

''You all right?''

''Fine,'' Josie fibbed, not wanting to even voice the hideous thoughts aloud.

He eyed her speculatively for a moment, then apparently decided to let the matter drop. ''Maybe I ought to take a look at the money clip. See if it triggers anything.''

''It's in the bedroom. I put it in the armoire, the first drawer on the left.''

He disappeared down the hall, and when he returned a few moments later, the gun was tucked inside the waistband of his jeans, and the money clip was in his palm. A scowl marred his face.

''What's wrong?''

When he lifted his gaze to hers, his eyes were dark,

stormy. "I think we can rule out that theory about me being a soldier."

"Why?"

"Besides the fact that I wasn't wearing a uniform, I can tell you that this gun is definitely not standard military issue. It's a Glock. Most of the time cops use them."

She didn't ask how he knew such a thing. Instead she suggested, "Maybe you're a policeman, then."

He shook his head, and withdrew the wad of bills. "No cop I ever heard of walks around with ten grand as pocket change."

"Ten thousand? Dollars?" she asked, barely able to get the words out.

"Yeah." He fanned the edges of the bills with his thumb as though it were a deck of cards. "Give or take a few hundred."

"Ten thousand dollars," Josie repeated, staggered by the figure. Granted, she'd known he'd had a lot of cash on him, had seen the large denomination on the bills, even wondered if they were real. But she'd never realized it amounted to so much. "But why would you be carrying around that much cash?" she asked, not realizing she'd voiced her thoughts until the words were out.

"I'm wondering the same thing."

Blake was still wondering why he'd been carrying so much cash later as he stared out the window of the farmhouse. His thoughts turned inward, he barely noticed the angry sky that continued to dump rain into the yard, turning the area into one giant mud puddle. Where *had* the money come from? And why had he been carrying a Glock equipped with a silencer?

Whatever the answers, they remained locked in a past he couldn't remember. Or had deliberately blocked out? Sighing, Blake leaned his forehead against the window. He closed his eyes, and the chill of the glass surface seeped through the gauze bandage to cool his skin. Once again, his thoughts returned to the money and its implications. The answers were locked in his memory, he reasoned. Somehow he had to find a way to access them.

He was still searching for those answers when suddenly a hazy image flickered across his shuttered lids. The image of a man, dressed all in black, who stood on a dark cliff in the moonlight. A strong wind whipped around him, carrying with it the sound of the surf crashing against the jagged rocks that stretched out below.

Blake tensed. Adrenaline pumped through his system, and he braced his hands against the window. A sense of urgency, of danger rushed through him, making his heart pound, his senses sharpen. Then suddenly, as though a door had been flung open, he could see the face of the man. It was his face. He was barking out orders in what sounded like French, but wasn't, and passing out hundred-dollar bills to men in uniforms with strange insignias on their sleeves.

Then just as quickly as the door had opened, it slammed shut, and the images began to fade. Try as he might, Blake couldn't hold on to them. His pulse still racing, he opened his eyes and lifted his head. But instead of the dark cliffs and foreign soldiers, he saw only the dreary, rain-soaked yard of Josie's farm.

What did it mean? Was it just a crazy dream? Or was it an actual memory of something that had happened? How had he understood the strange tongue? More important, what kind of business was he involved in that required him to meet with foreign militia at night?

"Just what I need, more questions without answers," he muttered, raking a hand through his hair, only to flinch when his fingers brushed against the bandage on his forehead. He swore. Why couldn't he remember the accident? And why couldn't he remember who the twins belonged to or who their mother was? Damn it. He wanted his memory back. He wanted his past back.

But his memory and his past continued to elude him. Frustrated, Blake balled his hands into fists, not sure which infuriated him more—not being able to remember anything or this sense of urgency, this feeling that there was something he had to do. Something important. But what? What? Maybe if he went back to where he'd had the accident...

That was the key, he decided. He would borrow Josie's truck and go back to the accident site. He knew he could maneuver the truck on the washed-out roads, and walk or swim wherever the truck wouldn't go. The water wasn't so high that his car would be submerged. All he had to do was reach it. If he couldn't find a wallet or ID, the car's registration papers would surely provide him at least with the answer to who he was and where he was from.

What about the twins?

Blake frowned. Until he knew who he was and why he'd had the twins with him, he would have to assume Josie was right and that they did belong to him or that he was at least their legal guardian. Recalling the way little Miranda had held out her arms to him, he was hit by equal measures of pleasure and panic. His relationship to the twins was just one more reason to return to the accident site. He needed to know if he was their father—and the sooner he found out the answer, the better. He was all set to go in search of Josie and ask her about borrowing the truck, when he recognized her scent. Suddenly the impatience riding him began to ebb.

It didn't make any sense. He couldn't even remember his last name or whether or not he was a father, but without seeing her or hearing her voice, he knew she was nearby. Roses and rain. The fragrance seemed to cling to her...to her skin, to her hair, even to her bed. Thinking of her bed, his lips curved into a smile. If he lived to be a hundred, he would never forget that expression on her face when he'd tumbled her into the bed on top of him. Desire licked through him as he recalled the feel of Josie in his arms, the taste of her on his lips. And if he was smart he'd put such thoughts right out of his head until he had the answers he needed.

Determined to do just that, he turned around slowly. It took him a moment before he realized that she hadn't spotted him in the shadowed corner by the window. Deciding to take advantage of the opportunity to study her more closely, he remained silent. Despite her efforts to tame her hair, dark strands escaped the braid and fell about her face. He thought of freeing her hair from the braid and allowing it to fall in long waves down her shoulders, over her breasts. His fingers bunched into fists as he envisioned all that thick black silk slipping through his hands. A male reaction he was sure, and one that Josie would not appreciate. He also doubted that she would appreciate the fact that he liked her long, coltish legs and the way she filled out those jeans and shirt.

Taking in her tall, slender frame, he wondered how she would look in a dress. The word *regal* came to mind. And he could imagine her reaction to that. From what he'd learned of Josie, there wasn't a pretentious bone in her body, and she went to great lengths to make sure you knew she wasn't a woman in need of a man. The question was, Why? She was young to be a widow, Blake conceded. And far too young to shut herself off here on this farm. Had she done so because she'd loved her husband so much? The idea that she might disturbed him. Josie didn't deserve only memories. She was a woman who should have a man in her life, someone to love her and to raise babies with.

But that man isn't you. If you have even an ounce of decency in you, you'll leave the woman alone until you know who and what you are.

The voice of his conscience was as effective as a slap, and he turned away to stare out the window once more. He may have lost his memory, Blake admitted silently, but he had no trouble recognizing the signals Josie sent out unconsciously. She may be wary of him, but she was attracted to him all the same. It had been there in those shy, yearning looks she gave him, in the heated response to his kisses. That old cliché about a moth being drawn to a flame came to mind and only added to his sense of frustration.

The woman had saved his life and the lives of the twins, he reminded himself. He owed her—big-time. The least of which was not to take advantage of the situation this storm had left them in. The decent thing to do, the right thing to do, would be to ignore those sexual sparks they kept striking off each other. "Easier said than done," he muttered, uncomfortably aware of the bulge already pressing against the zipper of his jeans.

"Blake? Goodness, I didn't see you. What are you doing standing there in the dark?"

Deciding to avoid temptation, he kept his back to her. "Just taking a look at the weather."

She flipped on a lamp somewhere behind him, flooding the area with soft light. "Looking at the weather or worrying about the money?"

"Both," he admitted, giving her marks for her perception as he turned to face her. How had she come to read him so well in such a short time?

"I'm sure there's a simple explanation for the money. You're probably worrying over nothing."

"I hope you're right," he replied, but at the mention of the money, all the questions came rushing back—along with that disturbing scene of him on the cliff and that nagging sense of urgency that there was something he had to do.

"Blake? Are you feeling all right?"

"Yeah," he told her, but a knot the size of Texas was forming in his stomach again, as more questions, to which he had no answers, raced through his head. *Who was he? What was he involved in? And where had he been going when he'd had the wreck?*

"Are you sure?"

"I'm fine. Honest. I've just got a headache," he told her, and realized it was the truth. His head really did hurt. Not only did the knot at the back of his skull ache, but the cut on his forehead throbbed like a sore tooth. He pressed his fingers to the bandage and frowned when they came away sticky with blood.

"I'm afraid it's too soon for you to take any more aspirin, but—" Whatever suggestion she had been about to make never got past her lips. Moving closer, she stared at his forehead, then snatched up his hand. Her eyes widened at the sight of the blood. "Oh, my God, your head. It's bleeding."

"Take it easy," he said, alarmed at how pale her face had gone. He closed his fingers around hers and squeezed. "I'm all right. I bumped my hand against the bandage a few minutes ago and evidently reopened the cut. It's nothing."

Pulling her hand free, she shook her head. "It is not nothing. It's a serious cut, and it should have been stitched. I should have tried to get you to a doctor instead of bringing you back here."

"Calm down and quit beating yourself up. You made the right decision. Suppose you had tried to get me to a doctor and been caught in the storm? What would have happened to the twins?" He waited a moment for the message to sink in.

"I guess you're right."

"Sure I am." But he could feel the warm seepage of blood staining the bandage on his forehead, and knew he had to take care of it or she would become alarmed all over again. "Besides this thing probably looks a lot worse than it is."

"I doubt that."

He shrugged. "Tell you what. Why don't you point me to the bandages and I'll change it?"

"The gauze and tape are in the medicine cabinet in the bathroom," she told him, leading the way. "I used an antibiotic ointment to fight off any infection the glass might have caused."

In the bathroom she took out the bandages and medicated ointment and set them on the vanity beside the sink. Standing behind him, she watched as he peeled away the tape and removed the blood-soaked gauze. "You got an old towel I can use? I don't want to get blood on your good ones."

She retrieved a towel from the shelf unit above the toilet and handed it to him. "You don't have to be polite. These are as old as sin, and we both know it."

"Thanks," he said taking the towel from her. Then he proceeded to clean the cut and dry it. Keeping pressure on the wound to stem the bleeding, he studied his image in the mirror. Heavy stubble shadowed a face that seemed chalky beneath the bronzed skin. The shock of dark blond hair appeared in dire need of a haircut. But it was the two-inch gash across his forehead that made Blake frown. Josie had been right. The thing probably did need to be stitched, but every instinct in him still said to stay away from hospitals, doctors, all official agencies. He'd experienced the same reluctance when Josie had mentioned contacting the sheriff's office to report his accident. Why did the thought of drawing any attention to himself disturb him?

"I was right. Wasn't I?" she asked, her voice anxious, her green eyes nervous as she stared at him in the mirror. "It really is bad, isn't it?"

It wasn't really bad, but it wasn't good, either. "It could be worse," he told her as he kept pressure on the wound. He could tell her how to stitch the cut for him, probably even do it himself, he realized, not sure how he knew such things. Just that he did. From the expression on Josie's face, Blake suspected it would be wiser and safer not to suggest either option to her. "It's just a nasty scratch," he informed her. "A fresh bandage and some more of that ointment should do the trick."

When he turned around to retrieve the ointment, Josie held it. "Sit down. I'll take care of it for you."

He did as she instructed, seating himself on the closed lid of the toilet. Josie moved closer, positioned herself between his legs, and tipped his face up to the light. As she ministered to him, Blake watched her. He noted the fine bones of her face, the sweep of dark lashes that framed her green eyes, the way her teeth worried at her bottom lip while she worked. In the confined space, he was painfully aware of everything about her—not only her scent, but the long line of her throat, the way her breasts rose and fell as she breathed. She smoothed ointment over the cut. Her fingers were soft, cool and should have been soothing. They made him restless instead, because he kept imagining how it would feel to have those fingers moving over other parts of his body. Aware of the effect such thoughts were having on him, Blake shifted. Using her teeth, she cut off the strip of tape she'd measured and bent toward him to adhere it to the gauze. As she did so, her leg brushed against his thigh, and Blake bit off a groan.

Her fingers stilled. "I'm sorry," she said. "Did I hurt you?"

"No," he replied, barely able to get the word out.

"There. All done." She took a step back and looked everywhere in that tiny bathroom except at him, making him wonder if she had experienced that same slap of desire that he had. "I probably should go check on the babies."

"Right, the babies," Blake muttered, making an effort to clear the lust from his brain.

She began to pack away the gauze, tape and ointment in the medicine cabinet. "I don't suppose you recall anything about their feeding schedules, do you?"

"Afraid not," Blake said, suddenly remembering that he had a lot of other questions that he still had to find answers to. And the place he needed to start was his car. He stood.

"Well don't worry about it. We'll figure it out." She closed the door to the medicine cabinet and started to leave.

"Josie, wait."

She stopped midstride and turned to face him. "Yes?"

"I know it's a lot to ask after everything you've done for me already. But I was wondering if you'd let me borrow your truck? I'd like to drive out to the accident site and see if I can find my wallet or some sort of ID.''

"Blake, I'm sorry, but—''

"Listen, I can understand your reluctance to lend me the truck, especially given the fact that I don't even know who I am. But that's why I want to check out the car,'' he explained, determined to get her to trust him. "So we can both find out who I am. You have my word that I'll be careful. And I promise—''

"Blake, it has nothing to do with me trusting you or not trusting you,'' she said. "I'd be happy to lend you my truck, but it wouldn't do you any good. The truck won't be able to get you there.''

"Why? What's wrong with it?''

"Nothing. My truck isn't the problem. It's the road. The creek bed overflowed during the night and flooded the main road that leads to this place.''

"I'm not worried about driving through a little water, Josie. And I'd be really careful with your truck.''

She shook her head and released a sigh filled with exasperation. "You don't understand. We're not talking about a little water here. We're talking serious water.''

"How serious?'' Blake asked, narrowing his eyes.

"Several feet serious,'' she replied. "The fact is, until the rain stops and the water starts to drain off, I'm afraid you're stuck here. We both are. You and I can't get out, and nobody else can get in.''

Five

She'd told Blake the truth. They were stuck here, trapped together at the farmhouse. And while the floodwaters had virtually isolated her and Blake, making it impossible for them to get out or anyone to get in, Josie couldn't help but wonder if somewhere there was a woman waiting for Blake and the twins to return. If she were the woman waiting for them, Josie admitted, she would be a bundle of nerves, listening for the ring of the telephone or the sound of Blake's footsteps at the door. And she would be growing more and more anxious by the moment when neither came.

Princess Anna von Oberland sat on the edge of the couch in the apartment that had been her home for the past three months, growing more and more anxious with each tick of the clock, each setting of the sun. She willed the phone to ring, to hear a knock at the door and the sweet gurgling sounds of her late sister Sara's twins. Neither came.

Blake, where are you? Why haven't you at least called?

As usual, no answers came. Try as she might, Anna couldn't seem to shake the feeling that something had gone wrong with the rescue mission. Blake was now nearly a week late, and from the reports she had received, Gregory had yet to hear from his brother. Wherever Blake and the twins were, she could only pray that they were safe from Prince Ivan.

"What's wrong, Mommy?"

Anna dragged her attention from her worries and focused on her son William. Reaching out, she brushed the dark brown hair from his eyes—eyes so like his father's. As always when she looked at her four-year-old son her heart swelled with love. She smiled at him. "Nothing's wrong— except that you, my son, are growing up too fast." She ruffled his hair, then hugged him to her.

"Mr. Hunt says that I'm getting taller," he told her squirming out of her arms. "He says it's the Texas air. He says I'm a big boy."

Anna's heart clenched at the mention of Gregory. "I think Mr. Hunt's right. You're not my baby William anymore. You are a big boy."

"Oh what a big boy you are," Josie cooed to baby Edward who lay on the tea cart that she'd converted into a changing table. After securing the adhesive tabs on his diaper, she leaned over and planted a noisy kiss on his tummy. Just as she'd hoped, he gave her a sweet baby giggle. Laughing, she snapped his blue and white jumper closed. Then carefully she removed her braid from his tiny fingers, kissing the little hands from which she'd taken his prize. When he reached for her, Josie's heart did a nosedive. In the space of six days the little scamp and his twin had completely stolen her heart.

And unless she was careful, she feared their father would do the same thing. Resisting the urge to pick him up and cuddle him again, she straightened his socks and shoes. The task completed, she tipped her head to the side and smiled.

"There now. Aren't you the handsome one? Just like your daddy."

"So, you think I'm handsome, huh?"

Josie jerked her gaze to the doorway, where Blake stood watching her, amusement twinkling in his dark eyes. Heat flooded her cheeks, and her traitorous pulse began what was becoming an all-too-familiar tap dance whenever the man came within ten feet of her—which was often since they remained trapped inside the house due to the continued rain and washed-out roads.

"Why, Eddie, pal, I do believe our Josie's embarrassed," he teased, a wicked grin curving his mouth. He shoved away from the doorway. "Do you think she meant it? Does she really think I'm handsome?"

Rats, Josie thought, wishing she could take back that remark. But since this was one wish that didn't have a prayer of coming true, she tipped up her chin and met Blake's amused gaze. "Really, Blake. I'm sure you don't need me to tell you that you're handsome," she replied in a voice that sounded amazingly calm, considering the nerves jumping in her stomach.

"I don't?"

"I wouldn't think so."

He arched his brow in a way that reminded her of James Bond in those action movies where bevies of sultry females were always falling into the secret agent's arms. "Why not?"

"Because all you have to do is look in the mirror," she tossed back. Just as all she needed to do was look into a mirror to know that she was a far cry from beautiful. *Pleasant looking* and *sweet natured* had been the terms she'd heard used in describing her to couples who came to the orphanage wanting to adopt a child. But *pleasant looking* wasn't *pretty,* and *sweet natured* wasn't *lovable.* And since no one had ever wanted to adopt her, she'd figured out lickety-split that her pleasant-looking face and sweet nature didn't measure up. Not for prospective parents, not for cheating husbands, either, and certainly not for handsome men like Blake. A man who, more than likely, had a gorgeous wife to go with those twins, she reminded herself.

He pretended to study his reflection in a water glass. "I don't know. It's pretty hard to tell what I look like under this," he told her, rubbing at his chin.

But even with the heavy stubble shading his jaw and a bandage across his forehead, Blake would draw a woman's eye. And it wasn't just his face and body—although there was certainly nothing wrong with either. Amnesia or not, the man had an aura about him that made him difficult to ignore. She should know since she'd been trying her best to do just that for nearly a week—with little success. If anything the too-long hair and scruffy beard added to his appeal. "Take my word for it. You're easy on the eyes." Trying to keep it light, she added, "In fact, in the school where I used to teach, the teenage girls would have called you a hunk."

"What about the grown-up girls at your school?" he asked, moving closer.

"I guess that would depend on the girl." Picking up Edward, she hugged the baby to her like a shield and moved past Blake to the baby seat that sat on top of the kitchen table beside his sister's. She placed him in his seat and secured the safety belt, then proceeded to prepare their bottles.

Blake automatically reached for one of the bottles and began filling it with formula. "What about you, Josie? You think I'm a hunk?"

His question caught her off guard. He was in a strange mood, she decided. After several days of brooding and avoiding her, he seemed almost playful—more like the man who'd kissed her in the middle of the road and had toppled her to the bed that first morning. Setting the bottle aside, she retrieved two of the jars from the large stash of baby food and formula that had been stored in the diaper bags, and struggled to open the jar of spinach.

Blake held out his hand, and she turned the jar over without comment. He gave the top one hard twist, and the blasted thing opened. Another grin spread across his lips as he handed it back to her. "Not going to answer me?"

"Your ego doesn't need feeding," she said, shoving the jar of peaches at him. "The twins do."

Suddenly his playful expression turned serious, and Josie could have bitten off her tongue for the careless remark. "You're right."

But she wasn't right, Josie realized. She could almost see the wheels turning in his head, the questions running through his mind, wondering what kind of man he was. Was he the kind of man who needed a woman to stroke his ego? She could have told him that he wasn't. He was a good man, a responsible man. Otherwise why would he have assumed responsibility for the twins immediately despite his out-and-out terror of them and the fact that he wasn't sure they were his? And only an honorable man would have stopped that last kiss from going too far when she'd been overwhelmed by the passion that had flared between them. She wanted to tell him these things and put his fears about his character to rest, but from the look on his face she suspected Blake wouldn't welcome her observations.

Josie sighed as she watched him spoon peaches into the dishes. She'd faced the demons of self-doubt and loneliness for too many years not to recognize them in someone else. Blake was struggling with those demons now. She could have resisted the skilled charmer she'd first mistaken him for. But resisting this strong man made vulnerable by his uncertainties about himself was about as futile as her trying to stop the sun from coming up in the morning. "For what it's worth, this grown-up girl thinks you're a hunk."

"Thanks," he said, not even bothering to look up from his task.

She'd hoped the reply would coax a laugh from him, or at least a smile. It didn't. She was still mulling over her disappointment to lure him out of his unhappy mood when he handed her back the peaches. As she reached for the jar, their fingers brushed. And a sizzle of heat shot through Josie's body. From the darkening of Blake's eyes, she knew he had felt the spark, too.

"This isn't getting any easier for either of us, is it?"

"No," she admitted, not bothering to pretend she didn't know what he was talking about.

"Sooner or later something's got to give, Josie. I want you, but I don't want to hurt you."

"I don't intend to let you hurt me." But despite her brave words, she was no longer sure of that. And the realization unnerved her, frightened her.

"I need answers—for both of our sakes. If you'll watch the twins, I'd like to try to make it to my car. It's a long shot that I'll find any ID or that the registration papers will tell me much, but it's all I've got."

"You can't go out in this," she argued, panicked at the thought of him getting lost in the storm or worse yet, hurt again. "You're injured, Blake. It's crazy to even consider such a thing."

"I have to try," he told her.

"Why?"

"Because I need to know who I am. I need to know if you can trust me."

"I *do* trust you."

"You shouldn't," he said, frustration in his voice. "Because even *I* don't trust me—and I won't—not until I know why I was carrying a gun and all that money. And don't tell me there's a logical explanation. Because if there is one, I sure as hell haven't been able to come up with it."

The scowl on his face and the tension in his body told her just how on edge he was. "It's only been a week. Give yourself time. Your memory will come back."

"Always ready to defend me, aren't you, angel?" he replied, stroking her cheek. "Honey, if you have an ounce of self-preservation, you'd kick my butt out of here right now."

"I'm not afraid of you, Blake."

He caught her chin in his hand. "You should be," he said, his voice as dark and dangerous as his expression. "I want you, Josie, and I'm not sure how much longer I'm going to be able to keep my distance."

Her pulse scattered at his words, at the raw hunger in his eyes. She wanted to believe him, wanted to believe he could actually want her in such a way. And if she believed him, she would be a fool. "If that was meant to scare me, then you misfired, cowboy. I don't scare easily, and I told you I'm not afraid of you."

He released her, but there was no mistaking the cool censure in his eyes. She didn't know what to make of him. And she was terribly worried that she would read far more into the situation than she should.

"Let's at least be honest, Blake. I'm not blind. I know I'm not the kind of woman who drives men to lust. I'm just…me. Just Josie. And I know there's nothing special about me. I'm a widow living on a farm for Pete's sake. There aren't any men beating a path to my door, and there never will be. And if you weren't stuck here, you wouldn't look at me twice."

He was furious, if the ruddy color in his cheeks was anything to go by. "Obviously you need a new mirror," he said, in a voice so low and tight with anger that a chill chased down her spine. "And I can only assume the men around here are blind. As for me, don't even attempt to assume you know what I would or wouldn't do."

Unable to speak, Josie simply stared at him. She squeezed both of her hands around the jar of baby food to keep them from shaking.

"You want honesty, my 'nothing special, just Josie'?" he said, moving a step closer. "Then I'll be honest and tell you that I *am* lusting after you. And there hasn't been a single night that's gone by that I haven't lain awake on that couch when what I wanted was to walk down the hall to your bedroom and join you in that bed."

Words failed her. She felt hot. She felt cold. Her heart raced so fast that Josie was sure it would burst. She clutched the baby food jar even tighter to keep it from slipping from her suddenly damp palms. And despite the romantic flutter that went all the way to her soul, she'd be darned if she'd make a fool of herself—not with him, not with Blake. She simply couldn't bear it if she did. Pride had seen her through the worst of times. Pride would see her through this. "What you feel is the need to reaffirm life. It's a survival instinct."

He didn't contradict her. He simply waited, which only added to her uneasiness. "It's the situation that we're in," she explained with a calmness that belied the turmoil going on inside her. "Proximity and the fact that we're trapped here together in a life-threatening situation like this brings out the primal instincts in people. Your accident and the loss of memory have further triggered those instincts. Your need to mate with me is simply your way of reaffirming that you've survived."

"Angel, you really do take the cake! I tell you that I want you, that I'm within a breath of tossing you onto the nearest bed and having sex with you, and you stand there and lecture me about primal instincts and my need to mate to reaffirm my survival?"

Excitement shimmered through her at his words, at the look in his eyes—like he truly wanted her, found her desirable. And darn it, if she didn't want to believe him.

"How in the hell have you managed to survive all these years?"

His angry tone held the cold slap of reality and cleared away her fanciful notions. "Believe me, Blake, if there's one thing I've learned to do it's how to survive." And with a heart that always dove first and regretted later, she'd had plenty of practice. Despite the emptiness that filled her when she thought of Blake and the twins leaving, she would survive that, too, Josie promised herself. Miranda's whimper pulled her from her gloomy thoughts. "And speaking of sur-

vival, this pair wants to be fed. Or do I need to remind you
of the joys of being awakened at 4:00 a.m. when these two
get off schedule?''

The reminder of the middle-of-the-night crying and sub-
sequent bottle feedings should have cleared all thoughts of
Josie and sex from his mind, Blake reasoned. It didn't. Although the demanding wails of the twins had dragged him
from yet another disturbing dream, when he'd stumbled from
the couch to check on them he'd run smack into one of his
fantasies come to life—Josie all soft and flushed from sleep,
her hair loose and mussed, her feet bare. The cotton robe she
wore was as practical as it was old. But the sloppily tied belt
provided him with a front-row view of the silky, feminine
concoction that she wore beneath it. The hint of curves
shielded by that silk had him hard in an instant. So when she
gazed up at him with those shy, hungry eyes, he'd been
sorely tempted to part the robe and discover her secrets.
That he could seduce her, Blake didn't doubt. Josie was
attracted to him—a fact she gave away each time she looked
at him. But there was an innocence, a vulnerability about her
that touched something deep inside him, a part of him that
he suspected hadn't been touched by anyone or anything for
a very long time. He didn't know how he knew that. He just
did. And he couldn't shake the feeling that whoever and
whatever he was, there was no room in his life for a
woman—certainly not a woman like Josie. She deserved better. She saw herself as ordinary—a woman not likely to turn
a man's head. But in truth she was far from ordinary and all
the more special because of her strength and lack of artifice.
Suddenly an image of another woman, an exquisite woman
with long, blond hair, wide-set eyes and sculptured features,
who possessed the same strength and determination as Josie,
filled his mind's eye....
"I worry for Miranda and Edward," she told him, her blue
eyes filled with concern. Her gaze strayed out of the window

of the plane waiting to depart Obersbourg with her and her son for Texas. "They are so tiny, helpless. It is wrong of me to leave them like this?"

"Listen to me. You're not leaving them. You're entrusting them to me. You have got to get yourself and your son away from here. Let me worry about getting the twins out."

"But what if you fail? If the soldiers should discover you..."

"They won't," Blake assured her. He didn't need to voice what would happen to him if he failed—not when her eyes reflected her horror at that thought.

"I have no right to ask this of you. The risk to you is too great."

"You didn't ask, Anna. I volunteered to go to Asterland."

"I do not deserve your kindness, and I should refuse to let you take such a risk, but I cannot refuse, because each day that Miranda and Edward remain in Asterland, the danger to them increases," she said, the barest hint of an accent in her voice. "I fear for their lives, Blake. I keep worrying that—"

He caught her cold hands and held them between his. "Let me do the worrying, Anna. You concentrate on turning little William into a cowboy."

Her gaze shifted to the small, quiet boy playing with the toy horse. "Thank you. Thank you."

He nodded and released her. "Now, we don't have much time. I need you to describe the layout of the palace for me...."

"Blake?"

Just as quickly as the memory had come, it was gone. No beautiful blonde named Anna filled his line of vision now. Only Josie. While the other woman had been physically more beautiful and had moved him with her concern for the twins, she had not stirred his heart and body as Josie did. But Josie wasn't a woman who would play games with a man, and she wasn't a woman who would give herself lightly. When she gave herself, she would give her heart, too.

That's what worried him. Because no matter how much he wanted Josie, he didn't deserve her or her love. Not when all he had to offer were patches of memory that pointed to a less-than-stellar past, a past that could hurt her. Honor demanded that when he left this place, when he left Josie, that he leave both her body and her heart untouched. But sometimes, he decided at the all-too-familiar ache below his waist, being honorable really did suck.

"Um, Blake? Unless you want to wear that lunch, you might want to start feeding some of it to Miranda."

Blake jerked his attention to the baby, who was chewing on a fist that showed signs of a trip through the dish of peach mush. She angled her other fist for a second swipe at the baby food. "Not so fast, sugar britches," he said, moving the dish out of harm's way. "No two-fisted eaters in this house."

Evidently thinking it was a game, Miranda relinquished her tasty fingers to smack that hand into the dish. Gold and green yuck splattered on the table. Blake jumped back to avoid getting hit. "Talk about impatient females," he muttered while he attempted to wipe up part of the mess.

"Don't worry about the table," Josie told him, laughter in her voice. "It'll clean easily enough."

"What about her?"

Josie chuckled. "Her, too. You've done a good job with them, Blake. They're both healthy, happy babies."

She was again referring to the twins as though they were his. He started to correct Josie, but decided not to bother. He may not remember who or what he was, but he did know that whoever Anna was, she and the twins didn't belong to him. He had a nagging feeling that his life-style precluded a family—which brought back the question of who did the twins belong to and why they were with him. Miranda's baby jibberish derailed his questions. He drew his focus back to her as she attempted to eat the spoon. He smiled. "Like that, do you?" he asked and gave her another scoop of peaches.

From the corner of his eye, he spied Josie stealing a peek at his dish. "Is there a reason you aren't giving her any spinach?"

"Sure. I hate spinach, and this stuff looks particularly disgusting."

"Try alternating. Give her a bite of the peaches, then try the spinach."

He didn't see why the kid couldn't just eat peaches if that's what she liked. But following Josie's instructions, he offered Miranda a spoon of strained spinach. The little scamp spit it right out. After two more tries with the same results, he tossed down the spoon. "That's it. She doesn't like spinach, and I can't say that I blame her. No way would I eat this stuff."

Josie sighed. "She's a baby, and she needs the vitamins. Mix some of it in with the peaches, and then try to give it to her."

He did, but with no better results. "She's not buying it," Blake told her a few minutes later. "The kid's too smart to fall for it."

"Keep trying. At least try to get her to eat a little of it."

Noting a change in the gibberish noises Miranda was making, Blake swiveled his attention back to her—just in time to see her warming up for a sneeze. "Wait," he commanded and scrambled to grab a napkin.

But the little darling didn't wait. She sneezed, letting out a hearty "scheww," that sent a spray of strained spinach and peaches across the front of his shirt and the right side of his cheek. "Oh, God, that's gross!" Seeing no other option, he attempted to wipe Miranda's little nose, then snatched another mountain of napkins and cleaned the mess off of his cheek. Josie's laughter added insult to the injury. "Think it's funny, do you?"

Still laughing, she nodded. "Oh, Blake. You should

see...your face," she sputtered and broke into another fit of giggles.

When she straightened to wipe the tears from her eyes, he was ready and catapulted a spoonful of spinach mush at her. It hit her square on the chin. "I wonder if it looks anything like that?" The shocked expression on her face was priceless, Blake decided, and he started to chuckle himself. He was just warming up to a belly laugh when she fired a spinach missile at him. It exploded on the corner of his bottom lip.

"Oh my," Josie exclaimed, evidently surprised by what she'd done. "Blake, I'm sorry. I don't know what came over me."

He spit out the spinach—which tasted even more disgusting than he'd imagined. "What do you say, Miranda? Should we retaliate?" Miranda gave him a toothless smile and clapped her messy hands together. "I'll take that as a yes."

"Now, Blake," Josie said, scooting her chair back from the table. "You don't want to do something you'll be sorry for. Not in front of the children."

"You guys mind?" he asked, pausing to swing a glance at the twins before he advanced on her. "They don't mind."

"Blake, no!"

She shrieked and turned to run. He tackled her and they both hit the floor. Straddling her, he stretched her hands above her head, where he locked the delicate wrists in one of his fists. Feeling lighthearted and caught up in the silly mood, he adapted what he hoped passed as a pirate's voice, "Okay, mates. She's our prisoner now. How shall we punish her?"

Giggling, Josie bucked beneath him, her body pushing against the area between his thighs. He responded immediately to the innocent caress—a fact that she didn't miss. She tipped her gaze up to his, and suddenly the laughter died on her lips. The surprise and yearning in those green eyes stole his breath, and what started out as a game threatened to become a lot more serious. Fighting for control, he released her hands and started to lever himself away from her when she whispered, "Blake?"

He froze, every muscle in his body strained at the invitation in her eyes. The male animal in him screamed to accept her invitation and lose himself in her softness. But his conscience told him he couldn't. "The crew says I'm to let you go."

Her hands cupped his face, and he shuddered at her touch. He could feel himself sinking fast. "Funny," she said, "I could have sworn they said they wanted me to give you a kiss for them."

"Angel, we agreed this wasn't a good idea."

"No, Blake. 'We' didn't agree on anything. 'You' told me it wasn't a good idea."

"And it's not," he insisted.

"You're right. It probably isn't," she told him as her fingers traced the shape of his lips. "But being a good girl hasn't exactly paid off for me. None of those fairy-tale dreams I had of a handsome prince falling in love with me, of having a family of my own ever came true. I'm tired of being a good girl, Blake. For once I think I'd like to be bad."

He sucked in a breath as she planted a string of soft kisses along his jaw. With effort he kept his body rigid and his hands from reaching for her. "You'd do better to hold out for that prince, angel. I have nothing to offer you."

She lifted her gaze, met his eyes. "I don't recall asking you for anything. All you have to do is let me give."

Then she was giving, pressing her lips against his. Her kiss was shy and sweet and brave. Like her. When she probed the seam of his lips with her tongue, he tried to resist her and failed. He opened his mouth. Blake told himself he could control things. After all, they had kissed before. How much harm could it be to share another kiss with her?

But this wasn't just another kiss. She touched her tongue to his so innocently, so sweetly, that he couldn't stop himself from responding. He tangled his tongue with hers, touching, exploring, feasting. He wanted to give back to her some of the magic she gave him, to show her she was beautiful, desirable, special—not ordinary as she believed. He wanted to show her all of those things that he couldn't find the words to say. So he deepened the kiss.

As though she'd been waiting for some signal, she turned to wildfire in his arms, and her response dragged him deeper into the flames. Nothing had changed, he reasoned, even as he felt himself being sucked under. He still didn't know who he was, what kind of man he was, what in the hell he was involved in. But at the moment none of it seemed to matter. All that mattered was Josie. Here. Now. In his arms. He wanted her. He wanted her more than his next breath.

Any noble thoughts he'd had about being honorable deserted him. Honor couldn't fill this emptiness inside him. Honor couldn't make him feel whole. Josie could. He reached for the snap of her jeans, already anticipating the feel of her skin. Then he heard it—the sudden thud, the sound of glass shattering and the startled cries of the babies.

Six

Lord, Josie, what were you thinking of? And what must Blake think of you after you all but attacked the man?

She'd been asking herself those questions during the past two hours, and no matter what kind of spin she might try to put on her actions, the answer remained the same. Blake would realize the truth—that the plain little wren had stars in her eyes for him. Stars? Hah! Had it not been for the baby knocking his dish to the floor, she would have been begging the man to make love to her.

And what would you have done when he turned you down?

Staring at her reflection in the mirror, Josie pressed her fingers to her lips and closed her eyes as she recalled the feel of Blake's mouth. He hadn't meant to kiss her. She'd sensed his resistance, sensed he was holding back, until whatever demons restrained him broke free. Then he had kissed her. And he'd wanted her, too. The heat of his arousal pressing against her had been proof of that. But when he'd kissed her this time there had been more than hunger and need in his kiss, there had been a tenderness, a longing, as though he felt something for her. As though he cared for her.

Get real, Josie. Next thing you know you'll be convincing yourself the man's in love with you. Haven't you learned by now that those sort of fairy tales only happen in books? And that they always led to heartache for you?

Evidently she hadn't learned, Josie admitted, pausing at the entrance to the den. Because one look at Blake seated in the rocker near the fireplace with Miranda in his arms and her foolish heart plunged. The scene was right out of her childhood fantasies. She couldn't ever remember not wanting a family; she'd always dreamed of creating one. And here was Blake, handsome as any fairy-tale hero, sitting in her den holding a baby in his arms. Yearning welled up inside her so strongly Josie pressed a fist to her breast to ease the ache. She wanted, wanted so much for this to be real—for Blake and the babies to be hers, for her to belong with them.

As though he'd sensed her presence, Blake shifted his gaze to the doorway. "I think she's almost asleep," he whispered.

Toughening her heart, Josie pasted on a smile and walked over to him and the baby. "I can't believe you finally got her to go down. She was so fussy, I didn't think she would."

"Yeah, she was kind of cranky," he said with a frown. A worry line creased his brow. "She feels kind of warm, too. You think maybe she's sick?"

His concern over the baby did nothing to loosen those strings knotted around her heart. "What I think is that she's teething."

"Teething?"

"Umm, hmm."

Panic gleamed in his dark eyes. "Shouldn't we get her to a doctor then? I can try—"

"Blake." Josie placed a hand on his shoulder. "She's cutting a tooth, not dying. She doesn't need a doctor for that. It's something all babies do. Unfortunately, the parents have to suffer through it right along with them."

"But if she's hurting…"

"She'll be fine. Honest. Her pediatrician will probably prescribe something for the discomfort when you take her for…when you leave. In the meantime, just try to comfort her, maybe give her something to bite on besides your finger."

"That's it?"

"Afraid so. You should probably put her to bed now. Do you want to do it? Or would you like me to?"

"I'll go." He followed her to the extra room, which she'd turned into a nursery of sorts with a crib she'd managed to rescue from the attic, and the old-fashioned sleigh bed that she'd propped pillows all around to serve as crib rails. She motioned for him to place Miranda in the center of the bed. And before she put the wall of pillows back in place, he ran a finger over the little blond head. The gesture was so gentle and so loving, tears pricked Josie's eyes, and she could have sworn the fist that had been clutching her heart from the start tightened.

So much for toughening herself up, Josie thought. She swiped her eyes and quickly exited the room. If she wasn't careful, she was going to find herself foolishly and unwisely falling in love with this man and his children.

Josie, girl, have you taken leave of your senses? Why in the world would you pick a man like this one to fall in love with? Even if it turns out he doesn't have a wife, do you really think he's going to love you back? Not likely. Why set yourself up for that kind of heartache?

At the sound of Blake's footsteps behind her, Josie slammed the brakes on her thoughts. Brushing at her damp eyes again, she made an effort to rein in her oh-so-fragile feelings. She stared out the kitchen window at the shin-deep puddles that now dotted her yard and the water rushing over the road in a steady stream beyond her gate.

"I'm beginning to wonder if it's ever going to stop raining

or if we're in for another Biblical forty days and nights of this stuff.''

"I certainly hope not," she replied. "We don't have enough diapers to last that long."

There was a long moment of silence. "I know you said you had a lot of food stored up, but you weren't counting on an extra mouth or two babies to feed. Of course, I intend to pay you for everything, but how big a dent have we put in your reserves?"

Mustering up a smile, she turned around to face him. "We're okay. I have at least enough meat and vegetables to get us through another week without worrying. It's the diapers that we have to be concerned about. They're getting low. There's only enough for about another four days."

"Then what?"

"Then if the rain hasn't stopped or the road hasn't cleared so we can get to town to buy disposable ones, we're going to have to improvise."

"Improvise?"

"Make cloth diapers out of whatever we can find, which means we have to wash them after they're dirtied so they can be reused."

"Oh, God. Please let this rain stop."

"Amen," she said, and laughed at his pained expression.

In the blink of an eye, he sobered. "You've got a beautiful laugh, Josie," he said, cupping her cheek.

Suddenly all the nerves were back, but only worse, and her unwise heart was beating wildly in her chest. "I'd better see about getting dinner ready," she said and moved past him. In need of something to occupy her thoughts besides these romantic notions about Blake, she seized the potatoes she'd set out earlier to serve with the chicken.

"Need some help?" Blake asked from behind her.

"Want to peel and slice these for me?"

"Sure." He took the knife, the cutting board and the bowl of small, white potatoes she handed him and went to work.

As she seasoned the chicken, Josie's gaze strayed to Blake's hands. He had big hands, she mused, strong hands. When she caught herself wondering how those hands would feel on her skin, Josie knew she was in serious need of something besides Blake to occupy her thoughts. So after setting aside the chicken, she reached for the bread dough she'd set to rise that morning. She sank her fists into the soft mixture and began to knead it.

"Listen? Do you hear it?"

Josie strained, waited to hear one of the babies crying. "Hear what?"

"The quiet. I'd forgotten what that sounded like."

Josie chuckled. "Babies do tend to cause a commotion."

Silence stretched between them for several moments. Then Blake said, "I'm not sure I like quiet."

"You can put the radio on if you'd like. See if there's any update on the weather."

He made a face. "I'd just as soon not hear any more about the weather or discuss it. Why don't you tell me about you instead?"

"Me?"

He flashed her a grin. "Well, I'd tell you about myself, except that I don't remember anything about myself. So that leaves you. Tell me about you, Josie Walters."

"What is it you want to know?"

He shrugged. "Anything. Everything. Whatever you're willing to tell me."

"There's not much to tell," she informed him, relieved he didn't mention the kiss.

"Somehow I doubt that. But since you mentioned growing up in an orphanage, am I right to assume you don't have any family?"

"You're right. That is, I don't have any family," she replied. Or at least none that had wanted her, she admitted silently, and beat back the stab of pain the memories evoked. Taking care to keep her voice even, she related the events that made up her life. "I don't know who my father was. I was two when my mother left me on the steps of a church with a note saying my name was Jocelyn, and that she couldn't take care of me anymore. Until I turned eighteen, I was ferried back and forth between the orphanage and foster homes."

"I'm sorry."

"Don't be. I'm not." Pity had been the one thing she'd had in abundance growing up—from social workers to teachers to classmates—and it was the one thing she found most difficult to accept. It was the last thing she wanted from Blake. "I was actually quite lucky. I escaped that awkward phase most kids go through of trying to live up to someone else's expectations. The only expectations I ever had to meet were my own. No parental pressure, no one to tell me what I should or shouldn't do. No worries about letting anyone down, but myself. Like I said, I was lucky."

"I'm not sure most people would see it that way."

She shrugged. It was either that or spend her life feeling sorry for herself and blaming everyone else for the things that went wrong. Since she'd never believed that to be productive, she'd opted to go in the other direction.

"So did you learn so much about babies living in those foster homes?"

"I picked up a lot of it there, and the rest I guess I picked up teaching."

"You're a teacher?"

She grinned at the memory and made another stab at the dough. "Was. I resigned this past June to move here. This place used to belong to my husband's grandparents. He inherited it about two years ago. When he died I inherited it from him and decided to move out here. I like growing things. I'm hoping to make it a working farm again."

"If you don't mind my asking, how did your husband die?"

"In a car accident. He was taking a turn too fast and

slammed into a tree. I'm told he died instantly.'' She didn't bother telling him that Ben hadn't been alone in the car.

"When did it happen?''

"Just over a year ago.''

"Were the two of you married very long?''

"Almost five years.'' Five years in which her sense of failure had grown steadily and her confidence diminished.

"Happily?''

Josie's hands stilled on the dough she'd been shaping into loaves. She cut him a glance. "You certainly have a lot of questions today.''

He shrugged, gave her a half grin. "Just curious. You don't have to answer if you don't want to. Except for the fact that you're a widow who's kind to strangers with amnesia and who kisses like a dream, I know very little about you.''

The "kisses like a dream'' comment had the nerves twisting in her stomach again. "Ben and I...I didn't make him very happy.'' The fact that Ben had been spoiled and selfish didn't make her blame herself any less. "He'd been out partying with...with another woman when he was killed in the accident.'' When he said nothing more, Josie told herself she was grateful.

"I'm sorry,'' he said from directly behind her, causing her to squish the loaf of bread in her hands, since she hadn't even heard him move.

"Thanks,'' she finally managed when she got her heart out of her throat.

"Did you love him very much?''

Josie hesitated. "In the beginning I thought I did. But looking back, I think I was more in love with the idea that Ben thought he loved me.'' Because until Ben, no one ever had. What she hadn't realized at the time was that Ben needed someone to praise him, to take care of him and to love him unconditionally. Nor had she realized that having only her to fill those needs would never be enough for him, that he would always need other women to feed his ego and allay his insecurities.

"He was lucky to have you, Josie. Any man would be."

Swallowing hard, Josie told herself not to read anything into it. "Yes, well. I'm not sure Ben would have agreed with you on that. But enough of me. How are you coming with those potatoes?"

"All done," he said, and indicated the bowl on the counter, which she hadn't even noticed.

"Great." She wiped her hands on a dish towel and grabbed the potatoes. Turning down further offers of help from him, she kept busy, fussing with the oven, basting the chicken, putting the bread to bake. She suggested he rest or read a book. He chose to keep her company instead.

She knew he was trying his best to make her relax with chitchat about teaching, about the weather, about the farm. But how on earth was she supposed to relax when he kept watching her? Looking at her with those sexy brown eyes as if he wanted to gobble her up whole? And if the looking wasn't enough, he seemed to need to touch her—a thumb brushing a smudge of flour from her cheek, a finger tucking a stray strand of hair behind her ear, a palm resting on her shoulder, his legs nudging the back of her thighs when he came up from behind her to sniff the warm bread as she sliced it. All those hungry looks and light touches had her wired and feeling as though they had been engaged in foreplay. Her breasts were tight and achy, her pulse feverish, her body aroused and throbbing. The feminine center between her legs was damp and hot and needy.

Oh, Blake had looked at her before, touched her before, even kissed her more than once. She knew that he had desired her. But he'd been an injured soul, a lost soul, robbed of his memory, of his sense of self. He'd reached out to her because he'd needed someone to hold on to, an anchor to right him during an emotional storm while he tried to find himself again. And she had been there—handy, convenient, a body to hold on to while he searched for his footing. His kisses, his desire for her had clearly been the result of that need. It had been the male animal in him responding to the female. It had been just as she'd told him—hormones and proximity, the primal instinct at work, an affirmation that he had indeed survived.

Only now he wasn't looking at her like she was just any warm body to hold on to in a storm. He was looking at her as though she was a woman he really desired, a woman who was special to him. And when he touched her, it didn't feel like just a means of asserting his survival. He touched her as though he cared about her, cared for her—as though she mattered to him.

Josie. Josie. Josie. Do you really think a man like Blake could care about you?

Yes, her heart screamed back.

It was possible, she reasoned. She didn't even know his last name, but she knew that she was falling in love with him, that she already loved the twins. She could make him happy if given the chance.

Where's your common sense, girl? Where's your pride?

Obviously both had been washed away in the storm of Blake's kisses. Now she was left with the shaky realization that she had set her sights on a man not only out of her reach, but one who might not even be free. Not that it seemed to matter to her foolish heart, which was in danger of being seriously hurt and causing her to make an even bigger fool out of herself than she already had.

What she needed, Josie decided, was to keep herself busy.

And she did keep herself busy—and she kept Blake busy, too. Setting the table for dinner. Cleaning the kitchen. Changing the twins. Putting the babies down for the night. By the time she joined Blake on the couch in front of the fireplace with a cup of hot chocolate, she was exhausted. The temptation to snuggle up to him, lean her head on his shoulder was so strong, she nearly shook with the need. Anxious to escape before she did something to embarrass them both, she said, "You know, I haven't had biscuits for breakfast in ages. I think I'll go out to the kitchen and mix up a batch for us to have in the morning." She started to get up.

"Not so fast, angel." Blake snagged her by the belt loop at the waist of her jeans, and pulled her back down to the couch. "You want to tell me what I've done to make you so nervous?"

"I'm not nervous."

"That why you've been running around here like a rabbit with a wolf on its trail for the past few hours?"

"I had things that needed to be done," she told him.

"And cleaning the oven couldn't wait?"

When she didn't respond, he tipped her chin up so that she was forced to look into his eyes. "Are you afraid of me, Josie? I know I let things get a little out of hand earlier, and I'm sorry about that. I shouldn't have. But I swear to you, all you ever have to say is stop, and I will."

The doubts she heard in his voice, saw in his face ripped at her. "I'm not afraid of you, Blake. I never have been. Not even when you were trying to scare me off. The problem is that I didn't want you to stop."

He tensed. "You're not making this any easier on me, angel."

Nor was he making it easier on her. The fire in his eyes sent desire swimming in her blood. Her knowledge of men had been limited to her husband, but never before or during her marriage to Ben had he ever looked at her with such raw hunger, with such longing. That Blake looked at her in such a way now sent a thrill of pleasure through her. "I'm sorry."

"So am I." He dropped his hands from her face. "Hopefully, the weather will start to clear soon. Until then I'll do my best to stay out of your way."

Staying out of Josie's way was easier said than done, Blake realized, as he worked on the screaming pipes in the

bathroom two afternoons later. The small farmhouse made
for tight quarters, and thanks to the weather, escaping outdoors was not an option. He retrieved one of the washers
from the items he'd found in the toolshed that morning before
Josie had convinced him to come back inside.

Convinced?

Hah! For a soft-spoken woman with shy eyes, the lady
could give lessons in persuasion techniques. She hadn't argued. She hadn't pleaded or even threatened him. She'd simply zeroed in on one of his major weaknesses—the fact that
he felt responsible for the twins. By the time she'd finished
pointing this out to him, in that oh-so-reasonable tone of hers,
the precarious fate that awaited the twins should something
happen to him, he'd been ready to take a horsewhip to himself. His need to put distance between himself and Josie had
been no match to his sense of obligation for the twins. As a
result, he'd been stuck in the too-small house with the too-
tempting Josie all morning, and he had been engaged in a
battle with his hormones ever since.

Ignoring her shy glances and the awareness pulsing between them had not been easy. But for the most part, he'd
succeeded. Thanks to fix-up jobs like this one, he had been
able to escape for a little while and not think about Josie. He
hadn't thought about the sweetness and passion he'd tasted
in her kisses, or about how soft and inviting her body had
felt, or about how much he wanted her. He slid the washer
into place along the pipe joint and sighed. At least he'd managed not to think about her all the time, he told himself. Then
he remembered the reason he'd gone outside this morning in
the first place.

*Face it, pal. When you came out of the bathroom and saw
Josie with the baby nestled against her breast, the rain and
cold temperatures were your only hope of cooling the hunger
she set off in you.*

Recalling the scene brought back vivid reminders of the
previous night—of lying in the dark on the couch unable to

leep, seeing Josie slip out of her bedroom and head down
he hall to the bathroom. Who'd have thought that beneath
he lady's no-nonsense, practical demeanor lurked the soul
of a temptress? Who would have thought that the same Josie
who didn't wear anything but old jeans and drab shirts,
would sleep in a long, silky nightgown the color of a summer
sky? Or that the body the gown covered would be so ripe
with womanly curves? And who'd have thought that the
black hair she wore in such a tame braid most of the time
actually hid a mass of thick midnight curls that fell all the
way to her waist? He'd been rock hard in an instant, and had
spent the rest of the night lying awake, thinking about her in
that bed alone and wishing he could join her there.

Growing aroused all over again, Blake tightened his fingers on the wrench and concentrated on the task at hand—
fixing the blasted pipe. He checked a slip nut, gave the
wrench another vicious twist. But try as he might, he couldn't
get the sultry image of Josie out of his head. "Dammit, man,
get a grip," he muttered, and went back to work.

Soon. He said the word to himself over and over like a
chant. Soon his memory would come back. Soon the weather
would start cooperating. Soon his life would return to normal—whatever normal was. "And soon had better hurry up
and get here," Blake grumbled, or he was going to go stark,
raving mad.

He double-checked the pipe fittings and, satisfied with his
handyman's efforts, started to crawl from beneath the sink
when he heard Josie scream, then a crash. Blake jerked up
and hit his head on the cabinet. Swearing, he scrambled to
his feet. Spots danced before his eyes as he half ran, half
staggered out of the bathroom. "Josie," he yelled, racing
down the hall toward the kitchen. "Josie, dammit. Where in
the hell are you?"

"In the bedroom," she called out, her voice anxious,
scared. "Please, Blake. Hurry!"

The fear in her voice ripped at him. He reached the bedroom on a run, then slapped the door open. And he damn near had a heart attack when he spied Josie dangling from an opening in the ceiling by her fingertips. A rickety ladder lay on the floor with two broken rungs beside it. Swearing again, he was beneath her in an instant, holding on to her calves. "It's okay, honey. I've got you," he told her. "You can let go now."

"No! You won't be able to hold me. I need the ladder. Get me the ladder."

"Forget the damn ladder, Josie. That thing's about as sturdy as a toothpick. I've got you. Let go, and I'll catch you."

"I...I can't," she said, her voice little more than a whimper.

"Josie, let go," he commanded.

"I can't. Blake, I—I'm afraid."

Great, he thought, his heart chugging like a freight train since he'd heard her scream. His head felt as if he'd been kicked by a mule. "I know you're scared. But you don't have to be, because I've got you," he said, trying to keep his voice calm. "Feel my hands on your legs? No way am I going to let you fall. You can trust me, angel. I promise, I'm going to catch you."

She hesitated another moment. "All right," she said, her voice shaky. Then she let go, screaming as she fell.

Blake bit back a grunt as she landed in his arms. She clung to him, her fingers digging into his shoulders, her body trembling violently. "It's all right," he soothed. "You're safe now. I've got you. I've got you." A wave of tenderness washed through him as she continued to shudder in his arms. He stroked her back, murmured soft words of reassurance against her head, now buried against his neck.

Several seconds ticked by and her shaking subsided. When she finally lifted her head, the eyes that stared at him shimmered with unshed tears. Her face was paper-white. A streak of dirt ran down one cheek, and he longed to wipe the mudge away. Her bottom lip quivered, and his urge to soothe the tremor with his tongue was so strong Blake had to grapple for control.

She was vulnerable now, frightened, he reminded himself. But the adrenaline surge that had sent blood pumping through his system when Josie screamed had shifted direction and aimed for another part of his anatomy—a part decidedly lower than his brain. Having her body plastered against him did little to help his condition.

"Thank you," she murmured.

"No problem," he said somehow managing to get out the words. "You okay?"

"Yes," she replied, dropping her gaze to his mouth. The innocent invitation in those green eyes had him breaking out in a sweat. Knowing darn well he would do something insane if he didn't put some distance between them fast, Blake was trying to talk himself into letting her go when she kissed him.

It was no more than a whisper as far as kisses went, a simple brushing of lips against lips, a gesture of gratitude at his having saved her from a tumble. But at the touch of her mouth desire bit into him with sharp teeth, and before he could stop himself, he was returning the kiss.

Josie parted her lips, and like the outlaw he feared he might be, he slipped his tongue inside to taste her. She tasted soft and warm and vulnerable, and as wild and passionate as he remembered. For several heartbeats he considered giving in to the need clawing at him to take what he wanted, to lose himself in her warmth, in her softness.

When she slid her arms around his neck, sank her fingers in his hair, alarm bells went off in his head. That she would regret making love with him, he had no doubt. And that same sense of honor that had made him resist taking what he had no right to before made him lift his head and end the kiss now.

Her eyelids fluttered, opened, and from her dazed expression, he knew she didn't have a clue at how close to the edge she'd driven him. Easing his arm from beneath her knees so she could stand, he kept his arm around her back and released her. Slowly, oh, so slowly, she slid down his body until her feet touched the floor.

Before he could say a word, she buried her face against his shoulder, wrapped her arms tightly around him. Blake sucked in a breath at the feel of her body flush against his own. His fingers flexed at her waist as he struggled to hold on to the last threads of his control, growing more convinced by the second that he was indeed an outlaw, because that sense of honor he'd been determined to uphold was in danger of being kicked aside. Desire licked at him like hungry flames. His throat felt raw as he managed to ground out the word, "Angel?"

"Yes?"

"Unless you want to find yourself naked in that bed over there with a man who doesn't even know his last name, I'd recommend you let me go."

Seven

Faster than a snap, Josie snatched her hands away from Blake's chest. She took a hurried step back, then another, putting space between them. Embarrassed, not sure what to say, she hugged her arms around herself. When the ladder had fallen, leaving her suspended like a puppet from the ceiling, suddenly she'd been six years old again and scared witless.

The memory flooded back as though it was only yesterday. Of being goaded by little Tommy Peters to climb to the top of the jungle gym. Pride had spurred her on, given her the courage to make it all the way to the top, even though she'd been petrified. And then her foot had slipped. The fall from the top of those metal bars to the ground below had seemed endless. To a motherless six-year-old, the sound of the bone in her leg snapping and the sharp pain that followed had been terrifying. And just now, in those few minutes when her foot had slipped and the ladder crashed to the floor, she'd been sure she was going to fall, too. The terror that had gripped her had been every bit as real as it had been years ago, and even worse because she'd known to anticipate the pain.

And then, as though out of a dream, Blake had been there—rescuing her, chasing away her fears, his voice calm and reassuring as he promised not to let her fall. She'd nearly wept with relief when his arms had closed around her and he'd held her close. He'd been so sweet, so kind, never once making fun of her, never once raising his voice at her. Kissing him had seemed the most natural thing in the world to do. She'd wanted to thank him, to show him how much his kindness had meant to her. Only what had started out as a friendly kiss of thanks had linked into another and then another, each kiss hotter, darker and more dangerous than the next.

She could have resisted the skilled kisses of a man intent on seducing her. But she had been unable to resist the need, the loneliness she'd tasted in Blake. She knew all about loneliness, all about the need to be held close, the desire to be loved. She could no more stop herself from responding to that need and loneliness in him than she would have been able to stop herself from drawing breath. Suddenly she'd been all over him, wanting to ease that need inside him, wanting to banish that loneliness. And she'd made a fool of herself. Would have made an even greater fool of herself, she realized, if Blake hadn't put a halt to things.

"Angel, do you even have a clue what you were inviting just now?" he demanded.

She had a pretty good idea, and some reckless part of her soul wished he hadn't stopped. She cleared her throat, forced her gaze up to meet his. "I just wanted to thank you. Heights scare me silly, have since I was a kid. And I thought for sure I was going to go splat all over the floor. Then you were here, and I was so relieved, and I...I wanted to show you how grateful I was."

"Yeah, well, next time try a simple thank-you." He let out a breath. Some of the stiffness in his body seemed to ease. "Listen, I'm trying really hard to do the right thing here, and I'm not sure that doing what's right comes naturally to me."

"It does," she assured him. Watching him with the twins had told her as much. "I may not know who you are or even your last name, but I do know what you are. You're a good man, Blake."

"Don't be so sure about that, because I'm sure as hell not. In fact, I'm beginning to think that I may not be a nice guy at all."

Narrowing her eyes, she studied him more closely. "Why? Have you remembered something? Has your memory started to come back?"

"I don't know if you would call it memories. It's more like flashbacks. I'd swear it was just a bad dream, only I've been awake when I get these…these glimpses."

"Glimpses?"

"Of me, other people, places. Faces and places I don't recognize. Doing and saying strange things that make no sense to me."

"What kind of strange things?"

His expression grew hard, bleak. "Strange things that your everyday nice guy wouldn't do. You'd be wise to remember that and not be so damn trusting," he warned. He moved a fraction closer, stared at her from eyes that had gone dark and dangerous. "Don't count on me being a nice guy, Josie, because chances are I'm not. Understand?"

"All right," she told him, positive he wanted to scare her, and just as determined that she wouldn't let him do so.

He scowled at her, obviously not satisfied by her response. "I mean it. You keep looking at me through those rose-colored glasses of yours, and you'll end up being disappointed."

And hurt when you leave? One thing was sure, she wouldn't forget him. How could she? No man had ever kissed her the way Blake had, as though he thought she was beautiful. As though he wanted to devour her inch by inch. Her toes curled inside her boots again now at the memory of that kiss. But, judging from the way he stalked across the room to inspect her crippled ladder, Josie decided it might be best to keep that bit of information to herself. "Can it be fixed?" she asked.

"I don't recommend it. The thing's rotten. I'm surprised you even made it up to the attic," he said, frowning. "Speaking of which, what were you doing up there in the first place?"

"Since the last tenants of the house left the crib, I thought they might have left some other baby things up there that we could use. I thought I remembered seeing a playpen up there when I first moved in, and it would be nice if Edward and Miranda could use it. You know, so that they'd have a place besides their car seats or the floor where we could let them play."

"We're not going to be here that much longer. As soon as this weather clears, we'll get out of your hair."

"You heard the radio. They're predicting more rain. Anyway, the playpen seemed like a good idea at the time."

He sighed. "It still is. But you should have asked me to get it for you."

"Yes, well, I've been trying to conquer my fear of heights. I thought I could handle this." And she'd nearly succeeded, too. She'd only had to stop a half-dozen times, sucking in air, talking herself into climbing up the rest of the way.

"Considering the shape this thing's in," he said, pushing to his feet, "it's a wonder you didn't fall and break your neck the first time you used it."

Josie shuddered at the vision of herself sprawled on the floor, her bones broken. At his questioning look, she explained, "I took a tumble as a kid, and it left a lasting impression."

"I'll bet."

But his expression softened, and for a moment Josie

thought he was going to fold his arms around her. When he shoved his hands into his pockets instead, she told herself she had no right to feel disappointed. What did she expect? Besides, she was an idiot to invite that kind of trouble. The man had *heartbreaker* written all over him, and she'd do well to remember that.

"Falling can be scary stuff for a kid."

He didn't know the half of it, Josie thought, remembering how she'd longed to have a mother's arms around her to soothe her fears. "It can be scary stuff when you're a big person, too," she reminded him, poking fun at herself. "I'd say from that bump on your nose that you've taken a few tumbles yourself."

Suddenly that shuttered look came over his face again. "I guess I won't know until my memory comes back."

Josie wanted to bite off her tongue. "I'm sorry. That was terribly insensitive of me."

He shrugged. "No big deal."

But she suspected it was a big deal. "Give yourself time. You'll remember soon enough. And when the phone lines are working again, we'll call the sheriffs in Midland and Royal. They're the two nearest towns. Someone's bound to be looking for you and the twins there, and will be able to identify you."

"Sure," he said, but somehow she didn't think he believed her. Worse, she had the strongest feeling that it wasn't just his inability to remember that was bothering him.

Had he remembered more than he'd told her? Like who the mysterious Lily was? Whether or not she was his wife? The idea hit Josie's stomach like a lead balloon.

"Don't worry about the playpen. I'll get it down for you."

"But the ladder—"

"There's another one out in the toolshed. It looked in better shape than this one. I'll check it out and then get the playpen down."

A soft cry came from down the hall, and within moments

a second wail joined in the fray. "All right," she told him and started for the door. She paused a second and looked back at him. "Thanks again for coming to my rescue."

"No problem."

"And, Blake?"

He shifted his attention from the broken ladder he was lifting. "Yeah?"

"I meant what I said. Give yourself time. Your memory will come back soon. Those flashbacks you're having are probably a good sign."

He didn't think the flashbacks were a good sign, Blake decided, several hours later as he tightened the last bolt on the playpen. He stared at the guard rail and tried to make sense out of the lightning-fast picture that had sliced into his consciousness earlier. Squeezing his eyes shut, he could almost see the scene again.

"Hurry, mon ami. The guards will be here any minute!"

"Go back to the boat," Blake ordered as he strapped two packs to the other man's back and urged him to the end of the balcony.

The man swung one leg over the balcony's rail and hesitated. "What about you?" he asked, his French accent pronounced.

A sliver of moonlight cut through the canopy of tree branches to illuminate the man's face. It was streaked with black that blended with the night and the dark camouflage garb he wore. Blake would easily have missed him were it not for the blue of his eyes and the flash of white teeth. "Don't worry about me. I'll try to delay the guards. When you reach the boat, give me ten minutes. If I'm not there by then, leave without me. Use the number I gave you and contact Greg."

"But, mon ami—"

"Do it," Blake commanded.

The other man didn't argue. Within seconds he disap-

peared over the side of the balcony, and Blake returned to the room and went to work. He didn't turn on any lights, but somehow managed to see in the darkness to turn over chairs, drag an urn out to the center of the floor, scatter heavy books and art objects along the path that led to the balcony doors. Footsteps sounded down the hall from the opulent bedroom. He could hear doors bursting open nearby, orders clipped out in that strange tongue. Blake slipped outside onto the balcony and shut the doors behind him. Quickly he inserted a device where the doors met and set a timing mechanism.

And then he ran.

Snagging the rope that hung from the balcony rail, Blake heard the commotion outside the bedroom door, several loud thuds as they tried to open it, then the sound of the door crashing open. Angry orders and shouts were followed by oomphs and curses as they came inside the room he'd booby-trapped. Grinning, Blake swung his legs over the railing as the intruders attacked the balcony doors.

"Break it down," a deep, menacing voice ordered.

Not wasting any time, Blake scrambled down the side of the stone wall in the dark. He heard the doors give and jumped the last eight feet, tucking his body and rolling to soften his fall. Charging to his feet, he grabbed the rope and, with a flick of his wrist the line and hook came free. He pressed a switch, and both line and hook zinged back into the metal box anchored at his waist. A blast sounded, and the impact sent Blake sprawling as chunks of stone and glass spat out from above him. Cries of pain and curses rang out in the night air as he hurried to his feet and started to run.

"Find them," an angry voice ordered.

Not bothering to look back, Blake glanced at his watch. Five minutes. He pumped his legs for more speed.

"There he is! Over there!"

Damn, they'd spotted him. Running flat-out across the grounds, Blake headed for the massive stone wall that surrounded the palace. As he approached the wall, he removed the gadget from his belt and aimed it at the wall. The grappling hook and line fired out like a bullet, whistling through the air. The teeth snared the corner of a stone spike. Barely slowing down, Blake began to scale the wall. A quick glance over his shoulder revealed at least a dozen soldiers pounding across the turf after him. Two other figures on horseback, hooves flying in the night, cut away from the rest of the pack and charged in front of the others, racing toward him and the wall.

"I want him dead," the tallest of the riders called out to the other man, who was just ahead of him and nearly at the wall.

Fist over fist, his chest tight from his exertions and the high altitude, Blake pushed himself harder. A bullet sang out near his ear, bit off a piece of the stone spike adjacent to him.

"Kill him," that menacing voice shouted again—closer this time, as the second rider drew nearer. "And this time, don't miss, or I'll kill you!"

The threat was colder than any winter he could remember and made the blood in Blake's veins run cold. He caught the top of the stone spike and launched himself up onto the top of the wall. Then he whipped a glance back at the man who'd given the order for his death. For the space of a heartbeat, Blake met those dark eyes and knew he stared into the face of pure evil.

Another bullet whizzed by his head, spurring Blake to action. A quick look at his watch told him he had only two minutes to make it to the boat. He threw one leg over the wall, but the lariat hooked to his belt snared. The soldier aimed his gun. Blake tugged at the line as the soldier released the firing pin.

"Damn!" Blake snatched the gun strapped to his leg and fired.

Opening his eyes, Blake washed a hand down his sweat-dampened face. Was it all a dream? The remnants of some nightmare? Or had he actually killed a man? More questions crowded his brain. And he wondered again who he was, what kind of man he was. Was he some sort of mercenary? A man who hired himself and his gun out for money? The thought left a foul taste in Blake's mouth and made his head ache. He massaged his temples, wishing he could remember, almost afraid of what he would discover when he did. But the questions continued to fire through his brain.

Are the twins in danger because of something I've done? Is that why I have them with me? And what about Josie? Would she be in danger now, too?

But the answers eluded him. Leaning over, he picked up the shirt he'd discarded while working and started to wipe his brow when a blinding pain seemed to explode inside his head. He dropped the shirt, sucked in a breath. Bending over, he braced his elbows on his knees and pressed the palms of his hand to his head.

"Blake, I wanted to let you know that dinner— What is it?" Josie asked, rushing over to him. "What's wrong?"

"Just a bad headache," he told her, the worst of the pain now passed. Unfolding his body, he glanced up, noted the concern in her green eyes. "I'm okay now."

"Are you sure?"

"Positive." He caught the worried note in her voice and wished she hadn't found him this way. He didn't want to tell her about the disturbing flashback, and he didn't want her fussing over him, either. The woman was a born nurturer with the survival instincts of a pea. Were he a robber, Josie would probably insist on giving him the keys to her truck so he could haul away the stuff he was stealing from her. He didn't want to steal from her, but he was afraid that he would. He knew she hadn't paid a bit of attention to his warnings to stay clear of him. Any minute now she'd be running her fingers over him, brushing a hand across his forehead to see if he had a fever, checking his wound, and he knew darn well that if she touched him, he would steal from her—her sweetness, her warmth. He needed a distraction—fast. Mercifully, despite the remnants of the headache and the new ache Josie always seemed to generate in him, his brain worked well enough to find one. "What do you think of the playpen? It cleaned up nicely, didn't it?"

A worried frown still creased her brow, but she directed her attention to the playpen as he'd hoped. Her eyes brightened. "It looks almost like new." She ran a hand over a rubber-rimmed edge. "You did a wonderful job."

"Just cleaned it up a bit, tightened a few bolts and refastened the guard rail."

"Well, it looks wonderful. I'll try it out on the twins first thing in the morning." She tipped her gaze back to him, and he caught the glint of curiosity, of sexual hunger as she looked at him.

Determined not to respond, he scooped up his shirt from the floor. When he straightened, her eyes were on him, roaming down his bare chest, lower. Desire fisted in his gut at her visual caress. Need trampled through him. For long moments he forgot about his concerns over his identity. He forgot about the unsettling memory of him firing that gun. He certainly forgot about his vow to do the right thing, the decent thing, and make no attempt to take the chemistry between Josie and him to its conclusion. He forgot about everything— everything that is, but Josie. He stared into those innocent eyes of hers. "Josie, I—" He remembered seeing himself fire the gun.

"Yes?"

He slammed the brakes on his thoughts. "I'm going to grab a quick shower," he said. Clutching the shirt in his fist, he headed for the bathroom, determined to cool off before he did something they would both regret.

Besides, he told himself as he shrugged out of his jeans and boots and stepped under the frigid spray, until he had some answers about who he was and what he was involved in, bringing sex into the equation would be a big mistake. And he didn't intend to make any mistakes.

"I will not tolerate any more mistakes," Prince Ivan Striksky snapped into the phone at the man he had charged with finding out who had aided the princess and the twins in their escape. Anger burned hot and fierce in his blood at his failure to find out where Anna was hiding.

"There is no mistake, Your Highness," the man assured him. "Our contacts assure us that the princess and the royal twins are not in Texas."

"Fool! Princess Anna may be merely a woman, but she is a clever one. Was not the plane that carried the twins traced here? She is hiding, I tell you! No doubt being aided by the brash American who helped her sister's twins escape." Ivan visualized the light-haired man that he had come so close to capturing. Hatred churned inside him for the man who had dared to take what belonged to him. Curling his hands into fists, Prince Ivan vowed to make the American pay for his insolence—with his life. And Princess Anna…oh yes, the princess would pay, too, for all the trouble she had caused him. He would see to that. And he knew just how tò make her pay, he mused, his lips curving cruelly. He would exact vengeance upon her for her impertinence where she would feel it the most—through her son and the twins. He whipped his attention back to the man on the telephone. "The princess and the twins are here. Now find out who Anna's white knight is."

"But, Your Highness—"

"You have your orders. Now see to it!"

"Yes, Your Highness."

Furious, Prince Ivan slammed down the phone and stared at his glowering reflection in the mirrored wall over the bar in his hotel suite. Midnight hair and black eyes stared back at him out of a face that bore the mark of his nobility. A blind person could see he was no commoner. He was a

prince. His Royal Highness, Prince Ivan Striksky of Asterland—and soon of Obersbourg as well.

"Damn you, Anna von Oberland!" He swiped his hand
across the bar, sending crystal glasses and bottles crashing to
the floor. He refused to allow the woman or the American to
best him. "Wherever you and the twins are, I will find you.
I will find you!" And when he did, he would destroy her
American champion, and then he would deal with Anna per-
sonally. And this time he would see to it that no mistakes
were made.

He had just made a big mistake, Blake realized. He
reached over to wipe away a crumb of corn bread from the
corner of Josie's mouth at the same time she flicked her
tongue to do the job. Her warm, moist tongue licked the pad
of his thumb instead, and the innocent gesture sent a blast of
heat straight to his loins. So much for the cold shower, he
thought. Mistake or not, he rubbed his thumb across that
pouty bottom lip. At her quick intake of breath and the open
longing in her eyes, Blake nearly lost it. He withdrew his
hand while he was still able to do so. "Josie, I—"

She pulled back, her dark lashes fluttering over her eyes—
but not before he'd seen the hurt and rejection in them.
"Where are my manners? Your wineglass is empty."

"Forget the wine."

"Don't be silly. There's plenty left. I'll just get the bottle." Shoving her chair back from the table, she stood and
hurried to the counter to retrieve the bottle of Merlot.

Blake shifted uncomfortably in his seat, grateful for the
cover the table provided him. How in the hell was he supposed to be noble and keep his hands off her when she kept
sneaking those hungry peeks at him? When just being in the
same room with her had him as hard as stone?

"Here we go," she said in an upbeat voice that was as
phony as the everything's-okay smile on her face. Her hand
trembled as she attempted to refill his glass, and red wine

sloshed down the sides. "Oh, no!" Flustered, Josie dropped the bottle, spilling the wine.

Blake grabbed the bottle, righted it.

"Oh my, I'm so sorry." She looked so lost and thoroughly ashamed, it took everything in him not to tuck her in his arms and hold her close. Snatching up napkins, she began sopping at the wine stain spreading across the tablecloth. "I don't know what's the matter with me."

"It's all right, Josie."

"I can't believe I did that. I'm such a klutz."

"You are not. I said, don't worry about it."

She kept her head down, continued to sop at the red stains. "Sister Charles Marie always did claim that I was in too much of a hurry for my own good. I guess she was right."

The words and the image of a younger Josie thinking herself to be lacking, tore at Blake's heart. "Sister Charles Marie didn't know what she was talking about." He captured her never-still hands, held them between his own.

She refused to look at him. "Did I get any on you? If I did, you'll need to soak your shirt right away before the stain sets. It—"

"Forget about the damn shirt." Holding her smaller hands in one of his, he used his free hand to tip her chin up so he could see her eyes. They were wide, filled with self-recrimination and shimmering with unshed tears. Her bottom lip quivered ever so slightly, and the telltale sign of her vulnerability ripped at him. "The shirt doesn't matter."

But she did.

He lifted her hands to his face, brought them to his mouth. One by one he took her fingers into his mouth and licked away the wine. He could taste the sharp bite of the Merlot, the softness and heat of her skin.

A breath shuddered through her. Her response sent another stab of desire rolling through him. Her hand trembled beneath his mouth. He could feel her pulse thundering in her wrist as he cleaned each slender finger with his tongue. "I promised myself I wouldn't do this,'' he said, more to himself than to her. He moved to her other hand, turned it palm up. He lifted his gaze, stared into her eyes for a moment, read the surrender and longing there. Every nerve in his body pulsed to life with need. Lowering his head, he pressed his lips to the center of her palm. She shuddered, and he repeated the ritual. ''You should tell me to stop, angel.''

But she didn't.

Instead she tipped her head back, offered him her mouth. Mistake or not, he wanted her. Shoving aside all the reasons he'd given himself not to allow this, he claimed her mouth with his own. He could taste the wine on her lips, on her tongue. He kissed her hard, then harder still as desire drove him. His mouth still on hers, he held her by her hips, backed her up against the wall. Holding her there with his lower body, he worked open the buttons of her shirt. Need burned inside him hotter than any flame. ''Josie,'' he murmured, as he slipped his hands inside her shirt to cup her breasts.

Beyond wanting, he opened the clasp at the front of her bra. The need to touch her, the need to feel her satiny skin, the need to know her, flesh to flesh, rode him with the speed and fury of the storm outside. He pushed away the silky fabric of her bra, then nearly lost his ability to think when she arched her back and filled his palms with her breasts.

She clung to his shoulders, her fingers curled into tight fists in his shirt. He captured the erect nipples between his thumbs and fingers and squeezed them gently. The sounds of pleasure she made had him shaking with need.

Josie tore her mouth free. ''Blake,'' she gasped, her body shuddering as he touched her. Wonder and excitement lit those incredible green eyes.

''Shh. It's all right, angel. It's all right,'' he repeated, even though her response was driving him closer to the edge. He could feel his control slipping, barely hanging by a thread. ''God, you're beautiful.''

He saw the denial snap into her eyes, kissed her before

she could tell him she wasn't. He knew she thought she was ordinary. She said so in the way she dressed, in the way she lived, in the way she wore her hair and shunned makeup. She was wrong. What the foolish woman failed to see was that she didn't need lipsticks and paints or fancy clothes to make her beautiful. She had an inner beauty, an inner goodness, that shone through strong and bright and made her all the more beautiful because of it. The fact that he'd tapped into the romantic, passionate soul she tried so hard to hide from the rest of the world only made her more special and more desirable to him.

He caressed her breasts again, and another moan escaped her lips. She arched her back. Lightning flashed outside of the window, illuminating her face, the pale skin of her throat, her long narrow torso. Desire, already a fever in his blood, exploded inside him. He'd promised her he would stop. And he fully intended to do so. He'd promised himself he'd only take a taste of her, and a taste wouldn't hurt either of them.

Only he wanted so much more than a taste. He wanted all of her. He wanted to bury himself inside her, to watch her face when he did. Fingers trembling with anticipation, with need, he ignored the alarms going off in his head and reached for the button at the waist of her jeans.

Outside, the storm raged. Thunder rumbled like an angry beast, shaking the foundation of the house with its fury. Rain slapped against the windowpanes like fists. But it was nothing compared to the storm of desire surging inside him. At last the button on her jeans came free. Need tearing at him, he kissed her again—deeper, longer, hungrier.

Surely he'd wanted a woman before, Blake rationalized. But even if he could remember any other woman, he didn't believe he could have ever wanted anyone as much as he wanted Josie right now.

Lightning flashed again, brighter this time. The blast of thunder that followed echoed in his ears, drowning out those voices whispering to him about sanity and honor. Until the only sound left was the drumbeat in his blood, urging him to make Josie his.

To hell with sanity and honor, he thought. He wanted her. She wanted him. He reached for the zipper of her jeans. And as his unsteady fingers closed around the metal tab, the world suddenly went black.

Eight

Desire still singing in her blood, Josie nearly whimpered when Blake lifted his head. Slowly, reluctantly, she opened her eyes. With her head spinning, her heart thumping wildly in her chest, it took a moment for her to realize that the room had gone pitch-black—and that she couldn't see a blessed thing. And except for the sound of their ragged breathing, the house was silent.

She wasn't normally afraid of the dark. And this certainly wasn't the first time she'd lost power since moving out to the farm. While the experience annoyed her, it never frightened her. So it didn't make a lick of sense that she would suddenly feel afraid now and instinctively reach out for Blake.

But she did.

Her fingers found his face. The stubble on his cheeks felt stiff, coarse beneath her fingertips. Fascinated by the rough texture of those whiskers against her softer skin, she shaped his jaw, ran her fingers over the sharp angle of his chin, along the sensuous curve of his mouth. She traced the smooth surface of his lips, found them warm, moist.

There was something erotic and reckless and exciting at being able to touch Blake this way, she thought. It was like being able to see him with her fingers instead of with her eyes. It made everything sharper, as though being rendered powerless to see had somehow heightened her other senses. Suddenly she was more aware of the way he smelled—that mixture of soap and wood and man. She was more aware of the way his body felt—all hard muscle and warm skin. She was more aware of the strength he kept so tightly leashed.

Here in the dark it didn't seem to matter that he didn't remember who he was or where he was from. It didn't seem wrong for her to touch him, to let him touch her. Here in the dark she could almost believe that Blake really did want her, that she might just be special enough. Here in the dark she felt less vulnerable, and less likely to disappoint.

Protected by the darkness, she felt daring and gave in to the urge to touch him and explore him as she'd longed to do. Remembering the sight of him earlier, bare from the waist up, the sheen of perspiration glistening on bronze sinew and muscles, Josie's fingers traveled from his face to his strong, wide shoulders, to his chest. His heartbeat raced beneath her fingertips, an echo of her own frantically beating heart. Encouraged, she slid her hand down to his stomach. The muscles there tightened, and she heard him suck in a breath. Then she moved lower.

Blake swore and captured her wrist. "Not a good idea, angel," he all but growled.

Embarrassed, Josie tried to jerk her hand free, but Blake's fingers remained locked around her wrist. She wanted to crawl into a hole somewhere and hide. Thank heavens for the darkness, she thought, grateful that he couldn't see her face. Even more grateful that she couldn't see his. Oh, God! What was I thinking of? What must he think of me—groping him like that?

He'll think you're a sex-starved widow.

Cringing at the cliché, a mewl of distress slipped past her lips and echoed in the silence. She tried to tug her hand free again, only to find herself trapped in his viselike grip.

"I'm sorry," he told her, his voice gentling.

"Let me go, Blake. Please."

"Not until you let me explain."

"There's nothing to explain." Nothing he could say would excuse her actions. Considering what a disaster she'd been in bed with Ben, her practically engaging in sex on the kitchen floor with Blake was almost laughable. Only she didn't feel like laughing. Tears burned behind her eyelids, but she refused to let them fall—not until she was alone. She finished straightening her clothes with her free hand and tugged her imprisoned hand again. "I need to go turn on the auxiliary generator," she told him as calmly as she could.

"The generator can wait."

"What if the babies wake up? They'll be frightened."

He hesitated, then released her wrist, but he continued to block her path with his body. "I'm sorry. I never meant for things to go so far."

His apology stung, but pride made her tip up her chin. "It doesn't matter. Please, I have to get my flashlight and go see about the generator."

His night vision was apparently better than hers because he had no trouble countering her move to step past him. His fingers touched her chin, tilted her face toward him. Lightning flashed through the window, giving her a glimpse of his stern expression. "I want you, angel. Make no mistake about that. If the power hadn't gone off and snapped me to my senses, I wouldn't have been able to stop. I would have taken you right here against this damn counter."

She remained silent, wanting to believe him, afraid to believe him. "Forget about it. I told you, it's no big deal."

"It is a big deal, dammit! I came at you like...like an

animal. I had no right to treat you that way. You deserve better than that.''

Taken aback by his self-directed anger, she swallowed hard and told herself not to read anything into it. Blake had been right when he'd accused her of looking at things through rose-colored glasses. Just because she was in love with him didn't mean he felt the same way. Her knees went weak at the admission. Oh, God! How could she have let this happen? He wasn't for her. She'd known it right from the start. So why had she done something so dumb?

The answer was simple. The man had been sneaking into her heart right from the start, calling her angel, demanding that she kiss his bumps and bruises. She'd taken him in like she would any wild stray, knowing full well the man was dangerous, that he might turn on her at any second. But he'd needed her and wanted her, and when he kissed her, she could almost believe he thought she was...special.

Don't do that to yourself, Josie girl. The next thing you know, you'll start hearing wedding bells and thinking the two of you and the twins will live happily ever after. Do you really want to set yourself up for that kind of heartache? Men like Blake just don't fall in love with ordinary wrens like you. Where's your pride?

Evidently her pride had been washed away in the storm of Blake's kisses right along with her common sense. Mustering up what little pride she had left, she prayed Blake didn't know how hard she had fallen, that he didn't know she was in love with him. It was pride that helped her keep her voice even as she said, ''All right. So we got a little carried away. It's understandable given the circumstances. No harm done. Nothing really happened.''

At his angry silence, she continued, ''Come on, Blake. I'm not some fragile, little rose who's going to go into hysterics or expect any declarations from you just because of a few kisses.''

''I'd say we went a little beyond kisses,'' he said dryly.

Josie nearly choked at the reminder. "So we did," she conceded. "Like I said, no harm done as far as I'm concerned. But if you still feel the need to apologize, then go ahead. Just get it over with so that I can go turn on the generator."

For a moment she thought he was going to argue further. Instead he said, "All right. Maybe I am overreacting. Like you said, nothing really happened."

A fist closed around Josie's heart, squeezed painfully and surprised her at how much it hurt.

"This time," he added, the words hanging in the air like a threat, like a promise.

Suddenly she needed to escape, to be anywhere but so close to him. "I keep a flashlight in the kitchen drawer. I'll get it and go see about the generator." Hurrying past him, she felt her way along the countertop to the drawers, pulled open the top one and closed her fingers around the cylindrical shape. "Got it," she said and flicked on the switch. Without looking at him, she started for the door. "I'll be back in a minute."

His hand closed over her shoulder. "You stay inside where it's dry. I'll go."

Her eyes darted to his face in the shadowed light. "But—"

"I said I'll go," Blake insisted, taking the flashlight from her. "I know where the generator is. I saw it in the shed when I was searching for tools." After lighting the candles on the table, he pulled open the kitchen door and stepped out into the storm.

Blake welcomed the slap of cold and rain that greeted him as he descended the stairs of the farmhouse. Frustration and unsatisfied desire churned inside him as he trudged his way through water nearly two feet deep to reach the shed out back. He hadn't meant to hurt Josie, but he knew in his gut that he had. He'd wanted her, desperately wanted to lose himself in her sweetness and warmth, to take what she had offered him. Yet he couldn't shake the feeling that he wasn't a man who led a life that deserved sweetness and warmth—especially not from a woman like Josie.

Yanking open the door of the shed, he aimed the flashlight inside. The beam sliced through the inky blackness of the barnlike structure. The place was cold, empty. Shadows lurked in every corner. Sort of like him, he thought as he spotted the generator high and dry on the cement blocks and headed toward it. After several attempts, the thing started. Satisfied with the humming sound, he headed back outdoors.

One glance at the house told him the electricity had been restored. He stood in the cold with the rain beating down on him and stared at the light spilling from the kitchen windows, promising warmth and refuge. He spied a silhouette of Josie pacing the floor, patting the back of one of the babies. The sight moved him, tugged at something deep inside him, made him want to be a part of the scene.

But something nagged at the back of his memory, told him he could never be part of such a scene. He turned away from the beckoning light of the house to stare out into the darkness. Some instinct told him that it was to the lonely darkness that he belonged. The wind whipped at his face, and he remembered another time when a different kind of wind had lashed at his face....

The wind whipped around him, stung his eyes as he struggled to free the grappling line that had snagged on the wall's pike.

"You fool!" The figure with the evil eyes shot his own man, then aimed the gun at Blake.

Blake cut the line hooked to his belt and jumped to the rocky path below. Pain exploded in his -shoulder, but he scrambled to his feet and headed in the direction of the beach. One minute. He had one a minute left to get to the boat.

"Don't let him get away you imbeciles! Get him!"

Three soldiers started down the wall after him. Blake hit

*the beach at a run. His lungs burned. His shoulder ached,
but he could see the water churning from the boat's engines,
and ran harder.*

"*Hurry,* mon ami! *Hurry!*"

A bullet zinged past, just missing his head. "*Damn!*" *Blake
dove into the water and started swimming to the boat. He
heard someone hit the water behind him, knew they were
close, but he didn't waste energy or breath to look back.*

"*Blake!*"

*He caught hold of the line thrown to him, and started hoist-
ing himself aboard. He'd be an easy target, but there was
no help for it. The man on the boat aimed his gun and fired
behind Blake. A man cried out, and Blake heard the splash
below him. Pulling himself up over the side, he fell into the
boat. Gasping, he ordered,* "*Go!*"

*The soot-faced man reminded him of a pirate as he sent
the vessel flying across the water.* "*That was close, my
friend,*" *he said, his accent even more pronounced than
usual.* "*What took you so long? I thought you had gone back
to pay a visit to the pretty mademoiselle who helped you get
into the palace. I almost left without you.*"

"*You should have. You're lucky I don't cut your black
heart out for not following my orders. You were only supposed to wait ten minutes. No more. Another minute and they
would have caught you.*"

"*Those dogs could not catch Jean-Luc.*"

*Ignoring the fire in his shoulder, Blake snatched up the
binoculars that rested near the Frenchman. He looked toward the shore.* "*Well, Jean-Luc, old buddy. We're about to
find out if you're right. Those dogs, as you call them, have
two boats in the water, and they're moving in on us fast.*"

Jean-Luc's eyes gleamed. "*Let the dogs come,*" *he said
arrogantly, reaching for the boat's throttle.* "*As you Amer-
icans say, watch them eat my dust.*"

Just what in the hell had he been involved in? Blake won-

dered. And whatever he'd been doing, would it come back to haunt Josie or the twins?

A door opened behind him, sending light spilling into the night and shutting off the questions running through his head. "Blake? Are you all right?"

"I'm fine," he called over his shoulder. "I'll be inside in a minute."

"What are you doing, standing out there in the rain? It's freezing."

"I just needed some air. You go on to bed."

He heard the door shut, and satisfied she had done as he'd suggested, he contemplated that conversation again. Once more the questions raced through his head. Who was he? What was he involved in? Were Josie and the twins in danger because of him?

He was so deep in thought and lulled by the sound of rain and wind that he didn't hear Josie move beside him until she tugged on his sleeve. "What's the matter with you?" she demanded.

"What in the devil—"

"Is nearly getting killed once this week not enough for you? Now you want to try to catch your death of cold by standing out here in the freezing rain?"

"Dammit, Josie. Don't you ever listen? I told you to go to bed."

She poked out that stubborn chin of hers. Her eyes flashed green fire. "Did you hit your head again? You must have, if you think I take orders from you."

The rain fell steadily, streaming down her face. "Would you please go back inside, and get out of the rain?"

"Not unless you come with me."

Blake swore. Lord, but the woman was as stubborn as a mule. Her teeth were chattering, and she hadn't even had the good sense to put on a heavy coat before coming out. "Go away. I want to be alone."

"Tough."

He stared at her, noted that her skin was pale as milk, delicate. Her hair streamed down the sides of her face like a curtain of wet black silk. Raindrops clung to her lashes, framing those defiant green eyes. God, she looked magnificent— proud, regal, tempting. He thought of the first time he'd seen her and had mistaken her for an angel. Only now he knew what this angel tasted like, the way her body would heat under his touch, the little noise she made when he kissed her. His gaze dropped to her mouth.

"Blake?"

This was insane. He was insane, Blake told himself. He didn't know who he was or what he was involved in. It was dark. It was raining. The temperatures had dipped into the thirties. And here he was, standing outside in the cold rain in water that reached his shins, and he didn't think he could make it back to the house, wasn't even sure he could draw another breath, unless he kissed her. He caught Josie around the waist, fitted her between his thighs. "Put your arms around my neck, angel."

Evidently she was just as crazy as he was, because she slid her hands up his shoulders, roped her arms around his neck. And then he kissed her. Softly, gently, he rubbed his wet mouth against hers. She made that sound, part whimper, part demand, and he felt himself start to slip. Trying to resist, to maintain control, he lifted his head. Her lips parted on a sigh. The soft sound ensnared him like a trap, and he swooped back down to her mouth. Her lips parted instantly. And he didn't seem to be able to stop himself from sliding his tongue inside to taste her, to allow her sweetness to warm away the cold dread that seemed to go all the way to his soul. He slid his hands down, cupped her bottom, fitted her to him.

Need stampeded through him. His heart raced like a runaway train. Realizing he was dangerously close to pulling them both down right there in the mud and making love to her, Blake forced himself to move his hands up to her shoulders and set her away from him. One look at her face, the dazed, hungry look in her eyes, and he nearly faltered. But he made himself tuck his arm around her shoulders, and led her back to the house.

Just inside the door, they shed boots and jackets in silence. "Give me your things, and I'll take them to the laundry room," Blake offered. When she shuddered, he said, "Why don't you go take a hot bath and warm up? I'll take care of the clothes."

Rubbing her hands up and down her arms, she hesitated a moment. Her eyes, filled with questions, with wanting, lifted to his. "A bath sounds good," she confessed. "You sure you don't mind?"

"No. You go ahead. I'll rinse up in the sink in the laundry room." Without waiting for her reply, he headed toward the other end of the house.

Way to go, pal. Nothing like giving the lady mixed signals.

He was a real jerk, Blake told himself, dragging off his jeans. He threw them into the sink. Nothing had changed in the past hour—except that he wanted Josie more now than he had before. He had no business putting stars in her eyes— and there had definitely been stars. He'd seen them. And he knew darn well that he was the cause. Swearing, he stripped off his shirt. Despite that cursed independent streak and the fact that she'd been married, the woman was as innocent as they came. She was too damned softhearted for her own good. He didn't want to be the one to bruise that heart.

But he would.

She wanted him. And heaven help him, he wanted to take what she offered. But until he found some answers, he couldn't—not when he didn't have even a last name or an identity to share in return. And from what he'd been able to piece together from the flashbacks, he had a sick feeling that once he did have those answers, nothing would change. He would still have far too little to offer her.

Twenty minutes later when he heard the bathroom door

open, Blake slammed his eyes shut and feigned sleep. His hearing was sharp, but he barely heard her footsteps as she entered the den, where he'd adopted the couch as his bed. But, Lord, he could smell her. He could live to be a hundred, and he didn't think he'd ever forget the way Josie smelled—that soft scent of a new rose opening right after a spring rain.

"Blake? Blake, are you asleep?"

Concentrating on keeping his breathing even, he remained silent and took care not to so much as twitch a muscle, when what he wanted was to draw her down beside him.

"Blake?"

She stroked her fingers over his head, her caress as gentle as the brush of a butterfly's wings. But he felt her touch in every nerve of his body. She sighed softly, then turned and walked away.

The light clicked off a few seconds later, and she was gone. For a long time he lay there, staring into the darkness, thinking about Josie, about the twins, about the disturbing flashbacks of him scaling a palace wall, looking into those dark evil eyes and firing his gun. His head ached from the questions that he couldn't find answers to, so he willed himself to think of pleasant things. He thought of Josie...of the way she felt in his arms, the way she responded to his touch, the way she looked so right holding the babies. His eyes grew heavy as he remembered how much he had wanted to be a part of that scene tonight with her and the twins inside the house. When sleep finally claimed him, he dreamed again, and as he dreamed, he could hear his own voice drifting back to him....

"Married? You've got to be kidding. Hank and Sterling both married? How the hell did that happen?"

"I don't know. I'm not sure they know, either," the man on the other end of the phone line said. *"All I know is that Hank up and marries his young, new secretary, and then out of the blue Sterling up and marries Susan Wilkins."*

"Susan Wilkins?" Blake paused a moment. *"Wait a min-*

ute. The librarian? Cute little redhead, nice body, lousy taste
in clothes and afraid of her own shadow? That Susan Wilkins?''

"That Susan Wilkins,'' the other man confirmed with a
chuckle. ''But I think the next time you see her, you'll find
her taste in clothes has improved, and she's not nearly so
shy anymore.''

"Well, I'll be damned. What's going on back there? Somebody put something in the water at the Cattleman's Club?
The next thing I know you'll be telling me that Forrest is
getting married, and that you're thinking about it, too. I
couldn't help but notice how protective you were of Anna
and her son.''

"You can scratch any notions about me and Anna. She's
a friend.''

"Uh huh.''

"Can't speak for Forrest, but given the herd of women I
hear you've kept company with, I think you're more likely to
make that trip down the aisle than me, little brother.''

Blake sobered. "I almost made that mistake once. I learned
my lesson.''

"Just because Lily—''

"Lily made me realize I have too little to offer a woman.
I made my choice. I'll live with it. Listen, the plane's ready
to go. I'll check in with you when I get stateside.''

"Blake?''

"Yeah?''

"Be careful. Besides the fact that you're my little brother
and I don't want anything to happen to you, a lot is riding
on this. You can't afford to get caught.''

Blake came awake with a start, the words echoing in his
head. "Can't afford to get caught. Can't afford to get
caught.'' Can't afford to get caught doing what? Sitting up
he shoved a hand through his hair. And what was the choice
that he'd made? Whatever he was involved in, would it en-
danger Josie and the twins? Kicking off the blanket, he

walked over to the window and stared outside. It was still dark, but the rain had slacked off to a drizzle.

He couldn't put it off any longer, Blake decided, regardless of the weather or Josie's objections. He couldn't wait for his memory to return. He had to find his way back to where it all began—back to the scene of his accident. A look at his watch told him that in another hour the sun would be up, and thirty minutes later so would Josie and the twins. But by the time daylight arrived, he would be gone. Knowing what needed to be done, he headed to the kitchen to write the note to Josie.

Josie was holding that note in her fist, waving it at him like a gun, when he returned later that morning. "I ought to shove this thing down your throat," she told him, and then shocked him with her vocabulary—which was extensive he decided, considering how much she knew about saints. Carrying the duffle bag he'd retrieved from the car, he headed for the laundry room.

"Do you have any idea how worried I was?"

Of course he'd known she would worry. He suspected Josie worried about everyone and everything but herself. He dumped the bag onto the floor and hung his jacket up on the wall hook.

"I was frantic! How could you just take off like that— without telling me?"

He didn't bother pointing out that he'd left the note. From the way she was strangling the thing in her fist, he didn't think she would appreciate the reminder. After toeing off his boots and socks, he stripped off his shirt and reached for a towel.

Color bloomed in her cheeks. Her eyes glinted with fury. When she stomped her foot, he bit back a smile. "But forget about me. I don't matter. Suppose something had happened to you? What about the twins? Who would have taken care

of Edward and Miranda? Did you even think about them
when you decided to take off?''

Her words hit the mark. Not the part about the twins, he
hadn't worried about them overmuch because he'd known
Josie would guard the pair with her life. It was the part about
her not mattering. It irritated him no end that she thought she
didn't. She did matter to him—too much.

"Well, don't you have *anything* to say for yourself?''

He caught her by the shoulders, and because he needed to,
he kissed her. "I'm sorry," he whispered against her mouth.
Then before he was tempted to kiss her again, he set her
away from him.

After a moment the glazed look in her eyes cleared, and
the fire snapped to life in them again. "That's it? You're
sorry?''

"Very sorry.''

"Of all the arrogant, bullheaded men. You go off in the
dead of night, leave me this note," she said as she waved
the thing in front of his nose again. "And then you walk in
here like— What on earth do you think you're doing?''

"Taking off my pants," he informed her and proceeded
to shuck out of his jeans. "I got soaked during my trek to
and from the car, and I'm freezing my rear off. I found a
duffel bag in the trunk of my car with some clothes in it.''
He looked up, found her gaze locked on the only part of his
body still clothed, and his body temperature kicked up a hundred degrees. "I also intend to take off my underwear. So,
unless you want to see me in my birthday suit, you might
want to march back out to the kitchen." Then he smiled.
"Of course, you're welcome to stay, if you'd like.''

Her lips thinned. She folded her arms over her chest, and
for a moment he thought Josie would call his bluff. And if
she did, he wondered how in the devil he was going to manage to keep his hands off her. He'd soon find out, he decided,
and hooked his thumbs under the band of his briefs. He
started to shove them down.

Josie whipped around quick as a wink. "I'm going to check on the twins, but you still have a lot of explaining to do, Blake. And don't even think about holding out on me, because I expect you to tell me everything you found out. And I do mean *everything*."

Unfortunately, *everything* Blake found out had only led to more questions. Questions for which he had yet to find answers, Josie concluded, as he slammed the phone down. "Still no luck?" she asked from the doorway of the den, where she stood with a fussy Miranda in her arms.

Tossing down his pencil, Blake rammed both hands through his hair and glared at the six passports spread out on the table in front of him. "Another answering service," he told her, his voice as angry as his expression. "Even the firm the car's registered to has a blasted answering service."

"Blake, maybe you should leave a message—"

"And who do I say is calling?" he shot back. "Do I say this is Blake Adams?" he demanded, picking up one of the passports and reading the name before throwing it down. He reached for another one. "Or maybe I'm Adam Blake. Or how about Hunter Blake? Of course, I could always say that I'm—"

"Stop it," Josie cried out, stung by the viciousness of his attack. Hugging Miranda to her, she turned away from him and sucked in an audible breath. She understood his frustrations upon discovering all the passports in the duffle bag with his photo, each bearing a different name and address. But understanding did little to ease the bite of his angry outburst.

"Aw, hell! I'm sorry, angel," he said, regret in his voice. "I had no right to take this out on you. None of this is your fault."

"It's no one's fault," she informed him. But his silence clearly told her that he did not agree. Based on those flashbacks he'd finally told her about, the foolish man was convinced he was some kind of an outlaw—a robber or merce-

nary or worse. Of course, it was ridiculous because Blake
was one of the good guys. She'd known that the first time
she'd seen him interact with the twins. No outlaw turned into
a big teddy bear because of a baby. And no outlaw assumed
responsibility for two babies that he didn't remember and that
he wasn't even sure belonged to him. Surely no outlaw would
be plagued by a guilty conscience, either. But the stubborn
man had a stickler of a conscience when it came to doing
what he thought was right. He also had a real hang-up about
feeling responsible for things. Evidently he adhered to that
old adage "the buck stops here." Only Blake thought everything was his responsibility, and the fool man blamed himself
for everything that went wrong—from the accident to his
amnesia. It was a wonder he hadn't tried to lay claim to
causing the crazy weather, as well. She could only assume
that he'd decided to lay that one at La Niña's feet instead.

He came up behind her, rested his hands on her shoulders
and squeezed. "I'm sorry for lashing out at you like that."

"I'll forget about it, if you will," she told him. Turning
around, she found herself and Miranda in the circle of his
arms. "I mean it. Don't go beating yourself up over nothing.
I know you're under a lot of stress, and I know how disappointed you must be after finding those passports and still
not being sure who you are."

"Yeah, well, I guess I should look on the bright side. Most
people don't get the option of choosing who they want to be
when they wake up in the morning. I do."

Oh, he was really bummed out, more so than she had realized. "There is that. But you know, there could be a per-
fectly reasonable explanation for you having those passports," she told him. From his skeptical expression, she knew
that he didn't agree. The fact that the telephone listings for
each of the persons on the passports led to an answering
service only seemed to confirm his belief that he was involved in something illegal. And the idea that he might be
was clearly eating him up inside. She didn't have a clue how

to convince him otherwise. Yet, she had to try. "It's true. There could be any number of legitimate reasons for you having those."

He flashed her a grin, but the denial in his eyes belied the smile on his lips. "Still determined to see me as a good guy, huh?"

"I'm only seeing what's there. You are a good guy. Maybe you don't see it, but I do. And so does Miranda. Don't you, sweetie?" she asked the squirming baby. As though in answer, Miranda held out her arms for Blake. "See?"

His eyes warmed as he took the baby from her, but he managed to keep his other arm fastened around her shoulder. She almost could believe he wanted to have her close to him, that he needed her. And although she told herself not to read anything into the gesture, she had a difficult time convincing her heart to listen.

"All right, angel. So what's your theory? Why would I need to travel with a pack of aliases?"

"You could be a private investigator working on a case," she reasoned, going with the first thought that came to mind. She caught her bottom lip between her teeth as she tried to come up with another plausible explanation. "Or maybe you're a government agent who's working undercover."

Blake laughed. "An undercover agent?"

"Sure. Why not?" she replied, warming to the idea. After all, Blake certainly fit her image of what an American 007 would look like.

He shook his head. "Honey, you're really reaching. What do you think, Mandy? Think our Josie's been sniffing too much baby formula?"

Josie's throat tightened at the "our Josie" reference. "Actually, it makes perfect sense. And it would even explain why you were carrying a gun."

Blake kissed the tip of her nose, then leaned his head against hers. "Angel, I'd like to believe that, but—"

"Then believe it," Josie insisted. She tipped her head back

so that she could see his eyes. "Why not believe you're really a nice guy? Why believe the worst?"

"It's called being realistic."

"Horse feathers. You're being pessimistic because you're afraid to trust anyone."

"That's not true," he argued. "I trust you."

"No, you don't. If you trusted me, you would have told me what you were planning this morning instead of sneaking out of here and leaving me that note."

"Please, let's not go there again. I explained my reasons. You wouldn't have wanted me to go, and you would have badgered me until I agreed to wait for the weather and roads to clear."

It was true. She wouldn't have wanted him to go out alone. As it was she'd been terrified something had happened to him and frustrated that she couldn't leave the babies to go search for him. "And what's your excuse for not telling me that your memory was starting to come back? Why wait until today to tell me the things you were remembering and worrying about?" she countered.

He sighed. "I told you. I don't know what I'm involved in, but whatever it is, I don't want to drag you into it with me. The last thing I want is to put you in danger."

"That's bull, and you know it." After taking the dozing Miranda from him, she placed the baby on the comforter in the playpen next to her sleeping brother. Then she grabbed Blake by the arm and practically dragged him into the den so as not to awaken the twins. "You know what I think?"

"No. But I'm sure you're going to tell me."

Ignoring his sarcasm, she said, "I think the reason you never told me is because you're afraid to trust me. Either that, or you're worried that I'll...that since we kissed a couple of times that I might..."

"Go on," he coaxed, a glint of amusement in his eyes at her tongue-twisted state. "Since we've kissed a couple of times, I'm worried because..."

Josie hiked up her chin. "Because you think that I was offering you more than friendship, and that maybe I was expecting more than friendship from you in return," she said, finally managing to get the words out. "Well, I'm not."

"You're not what? Offering me friendship?"

Josie glared at him for enjoying her discomfort. "I'm offering you friendship, but that's all. And I'm not expecting anything more than friendship in return." Just because she felt more than friendship for him, didn't mean he felt the same way. She hadn't needed him to draw a picture for her— not last night and not now. He'd made it painfully clear when he'd pretended to be asleep last night that he didn't want her—not the way she wanted him. The rejection hurt, more than she'd thought it could. But she'd handled it the same way she'd handled rejections in the past. She might be ordinary in a lot of ways, but she had more than her share of pride. She'd gathered her pride around her like a mantle. Only where Blake was concerned, her pride didn't seem to be much comfort.

"Friendship," he said as though considering the word. "Is that what you were offering, Josie? Friendship?"

Hugging her arms around herself, she held his gaze. "Yes. Of course, I'd be a liar if I said I didn't enjoy kissing you. We both know that I did. You don't need me to tell you that you're a great kisser," she said, struggling to keep her voice light when her heart ached.

"And you would know because you've had lots of experience kissing," he mocked.

"I am a widow," she reminded him, and she'd married the only man who'd ever kissed her or paid any attention to her.

"Ah, yes. How could I forget? You're an experienced widow, not some shy, innocent who doesn't know very much about men."

"That's right."

"And I certainly have no reason to feel guilty for almost taking advantage of you last night."

His self-mocking tone flustered her. "No, you don't. Because there was never a question that you would take advantage of me, Blake." She swallowed, knowing she was making a mess of this. "What I'm trying to tell you is that you didn't have to worry. You don't have to worry, not where I'm concerned. I knew things would never have gone beyond those kisses."

"You did?"

She nodded.

"You care to explain that logic of yours to me, angel? Because last night before the power went off, I seem to remember moving way beyond a few innocent kisses, and I have to tell you I don't remember hearing the word 'stop' pass your lips."

Heat rushed to Josie's cheeks at the reminder. "Because I didn't need to. And even if there hadn't been a blackout, you would have stopped."

"I'm not a saint, Josie," he warned her.

"I never thought for a minute that you were." A fallen angel perhaps, but not a saint.

He moved a step closer, until his thighs nearly bumped hers. "I wanted you last night. I still do."

Her pulse scrambled. Her romantic heart nearly beat a hole in her chest before she put a skidding halt to her imagination and remembered who she was, what she was. Ordinary Josie Walters. Not anyone special. Certainly not a woman for a man like Blake. "And we both know it's the proximity thing and your amnesia behind those feelings—not me."

She ignored the swear word he spit out and the comment about mule-headed women. But when he yanked her into his arms, pressed her against him, it was difficult to ignore his arousal pressed against her.

"I want you, angel," he hissed the words against her lips. "And take my word for it, it doesn't have a damn thing to do with proximity or amnesia." Then he took her mouth, captured it as surely as he had managed to capture her heart. When he lifted his head, he whispered, "Still think you can trust me to stop?"

Josie nodded because she didn't think she could speak.

Her response clearly baffled him, angered him. For a moment she thought he was going to shake her. "How in the hell can you say that after the way I just kissed you?"

"Because I know you'd never follow through on it—not as long as you can't remember. You know as well as I do that it took two people to create Edward and Miranda, and the chances are that the other person in on the project was your wife. You're not a cheater, Blake. You might kiss me, you might even think you want me, but you would never let it go further as long as there's a possibility that you're married."

"Well then, angel, I guess you have a problem. Because you see one of the things I did remember is that I'm not married."

Nine

Josie's heart slammed against her chest, stopped. "What did you say?"

"I said I'm not married. I don't have a wife, Josie."

"But, I thought…" The oxygen flow to her brain seemed to stall. "Then you remember—"

"Not all of it. Not my real name and not the things that I need to. But last night when I was checking out the generator, I guess it triggered some sort of switch in my brain or something, because suddenly I started to remember this phone conversation I had with a guy who's apparently my brother. He was telling me about some people, friends I guess, who'd just gotten married, and during the course of the conversation it became clear that I wasn't. Married, I mean. Apparently, I'm not married now, never have been, and I'm not engaged."

"I see," she said. And she did. Painfully so. He'd known last night he was free. He'd known, and yet he had still pretended to be asleep when she'd come to him.

Wake up and smell the coffee, Josie. He doesn't want you. Not that way. Not the way you want him. Where's your pride, girl? Where's your pride?

Evidently she'd lost her pride around the same time she'd lost her heart to him. But no point in letting him know that. No point in shaming herself and embarrassing him further. "But what about the twins' mother?"

He rubbed the back of his neck. "I don't know. It's one of the things that's been driving me crazy because, considering all the bits and pieces that are coming back to me, you'd think I'd remember those two and why I have them with me. But I don't remember them—which makes me think that I was right about them not being mine, except that..." He looked at her, bewilderment in his eyes. "Except that I feel as though I'm connected to them somehow."

"Probably because you are connected to them."

"Maybe. Whether I am or not doesn't matter right now. What does matter is what we do know about me. I was traveling with a half-dozen phony passports, a lot of cash and a gun, and I had men with weapons chasing me. In *my* book that all adds up to one thing—bad news. *I'm* bad news, angel. And there's no way you should let yourself become involved with me. Understand?"

"What I understand, Blake, is that you take everything way too seriously. Who said I was involved with you? Or that I even want to be? Is that what you think? All because of a few kisses?" she challenged, doing her best to salvage whatever pride she could. "All I'm offering is a place for you and those babies to stay until the roads clear, a few meals and my friendship. If you thought I was offering more than that, then you were wrong."

Maybe he was wrong, Blake conceded, as he watched Josie storm off. Or maybe the problem was that he wanted a great deal more from her than the friendship she claimed to be offering. He stood there several minutes contemplating what Josie had told him. He was still trying to decipher his feelings when he saw her with a twin in each arm. She said nothing, simply looked at him for a moment, then headed for the nursery. And then he knew. He hadn't been wrong, Blake acknowledged. His angel was lying through her pretty white teeth. What she felt for him was a lot more than friendship, and it didn't have a thing to do with proximity and primal instincts. She thought she was in love with him.

For someone with sharp instincts, he was apparently pretty slow. He'd almost bought the line she'd given him, and probably would have...until he'd seen her eyes. Angel eyes, the color of summer grass, and filled with the same shy yearning and loneliness he'd noticed the first time he'd seen her. But now there was also love in those eyes...and pain. Pain that he had caused. Josie *did* want him, even thought she was in love with him. And Lord knows, he wanted her and cared about her. Maybe too much. Because a part of him almost wished his memory wouldn't come back, that he could just stay here with Josie and the twins, take her love and try to be the man she thought he was.

But each time he recalled looking into that evil face, hearing that cold, empty voice give the order for him to be killed, he knew that he couldn't take that chance. Not when it meant putting Josie, and possibly even the twins, in danger. No. It was best this way. He'd meant what he'd told her. He was bad news, and the more he discovered about himself, the more sure he was of that fact. There were some gambles a man couldn't afford to take, and staying with Josie was one of them. For her sake, he would have to walk away, even if it meant hurting her.

But in order to walk away, he had to know where to go. More important, for Josie's and the twins' sakes, he needed to know who and what would be waiting for him at the other end. That meant he didn't have the luxury of waiting for the rest of his memory to return. He had to find the answers he needed.

Heading back to the kitchen, he tried his best to ignore the soft hum of Josie's voice as she crooned a lullaby in the next room. Somehow, some way, he told himself, he had to find those answers. Once he had them, he would get out of her life. It was the right thing to do, he reasoned. Just as it had been the right thing for him to pretend to be asleep last night and for him not to take advantage of her attraction to him.

"Hush little baby, don't you cry..."

But he'd be damned if doing the right thing was proving to be easy, Blake decided, as the sound of Josie's voice teased him. Snatching up the phone, he punched out the number for directory assistance. And as he listened to the phone ring at the other end of the line, he tried not to think about how sweet the lullaby sounded, or how much he wanted the woman singing it.

Yet call after call and throughout the rest of the day, he thought about Josie, wanted Josie. Even sometime after midnight, when exhaustion claimed him and he collapsed on the couch and fell asleep, he was thinking of Josie, wanting Josie.

Blake was still thinking of Josie and wanting her when he came awake with a start two hours later. He'd dreamed of being on the boat again, only this time as he sped away from the bullets and aimed for a distant shore, Josie had been on that other shore waiting for him. Sitting up, he shoved his hands through his sweat-damp hair. His heart still racing, he held his aching head in his hands, worked to slow his pulse rate back to normal. Once he had achieved that feat, he rose and started for the bathroom to get some aspirin.

Then he heard it—Josie singing. It was just the faintest of sounds, a few musical notes floating ever so softly from the babies' room down the hall and out into the darkness to him. Her voice seemed to call to him, swirl around him, caress him. His gut clenched at the erotic images going through his mind. He wanted to go to her, to surround himself in her sweetness, in her light, in her warmth. He gritted his teeth, told himself he couldn't. Turning away from the beckoning sound of her voice, Blake shoved open the door to the bathroom instead.

But the trip to the bathroom didn't help. Not only did he not find any aspirin in his search of the medicine cabinet, but when he opened the door to exit, Josie was still singing. Only now the sound had grown infinitely sweeter, infinitely more compelling, and impossible to resist.

Like the Pied Piper's flute, her voice called to him, drew him with the same powerful magic. He meant to go back to the den. He truly did. But his feet started moving in the opposite direction toward the nursery and the sound of Josie's voice. Pausing just outside the doorway, Blake told himself he just wanted to look inside, to make sure everything was okay with her and the twins. So he moved a step closer and glanced into the room. And the air backed up into his lungs. Pale light fell from a corner lamp, painting the room in an almost ethereal glow. The old-fashioned rocker made a gentle swooshing noise as it swayed back and forth. But it was the woman seated in that rocker who stole his breath away. Josie! With a baby's head pressed against her breast, she sang a soft, dreamy song about a sandman to the child in her arms. Tonight she hadn't bothered with the worn, cotton robe, and the satiny blue gown draped her woman's body. Her hair hung free, a waterfall of black silk that spilled down her shoulders and back, falling nearly to her waist. But it was the look of maternal love on her face that made his throat grow thick with emotion. She reminded him of Raphael's *Madonna and Child.* Only this was no priceless painting.

This was Josie. Josie of the shy green eyes. Josie of the musical laugh. Josie of the too-soft, too-giving heart. He wanted to go to her, to be a part of that beautiful picture before him. He wanted to have her look up at him with those shy green eyes, to hear the sound of her musical laughter. He wanted to lose himself in her softness and sweetness and warmth.

As though she'd known he was there, Josie glanced up, and her eyes met his across the room. Her gaze dipped lower, taking in his bare chest and pajama bottoms, before shooting back up to his face. But it was too late. He'd seen the quiet yearning as she'd looked at him. He'd seen the sensual hunger. His gut tightened instantly in response. When he could find his voice, he said, "I'm sorry. I didn't mean to disturb you."

"Did you need something?" she whispered.

Desire clawing at him, Blake beat back the urge to tell her that what he needed was her. He wanted to take her in his arms and make love to her now. But it was because he wanted her so desperately that he forced himself to remain where he was. He shook his head. "I was coming out of the bathroom when I heard you. I thought I'd better check to be sure everything's okay. She all right?"

Josie's lips curved. "How did you know it was Miranda?"

He shrugged. "Lucky guess. She's been pretty fussy lately."

"I know. But she's fine. Just a little restless. She's asleep now," Josie said, standing up slowly. "I was just about to put her back to bed."

With Miranda cradled in her arms, the neck of her gown dipped and pulled tautly across Josie's breasts, emphasizing their fullness and the dark rosy tips of her nipples. Swallowing hard, Blake forced his gaze upward. "I'll get out of your way so you can get back to bed. I'm going to hit the sack again, too, just as soon as I find some aspirin." He started to turn away, knowing if he didn't get out of there quickly he was liable to make a mistake both of them would regret.

"Blake, wait," she said in a loud whisper.

He cut a glance back at her. "Yeah?"

"The aspirin isn't in the bathroom. I took some before I went to bed earlier and left the bottle on my nightstand." She stroked a finger along the baby's face. "Give me a second to make sure she's down, and I'll get them for you. Or, if you want, you're welcome to go get them yourself."

"Don't worry about it," he said, dragging his eyes from the sight of those long slender fingers and the effect watching them was having on his body. "I don't need any aspirin after all. My head's feeling better. I'll just see you in the morning. Try to get some sleep."

But Josie couldn't sleep. She was wound up tighter than a spring. And, of course, Blake was the cause. Her foolish heart had stuttered when she'd discovered him standing in the doorway watching her earlier, but it had been the intensity, the strength of need and longing she'd seen in those dark eyes of his that had stunned her, touched her too deeply. He'd had the look of a desperate man, a man at the end of his rope. And it was that lonely desperation she'd seen in his eyes that haunted her now.

Kicking off the covers, Josie sat on the side of the bed, giving up on the notion of sleep. She couldn't. Not when her head and heart were in such a state of confusion. The house was as quiet as a church, something she'd never minded in the past. She did mind it now because she could hear Blake out there on the couch, tossing and turning. Evidently, he didn't seem to be having an easy time going to sleep, either.

As she wondered at the source of his insomnia, she recalled that tightly leashed control she'd sensed in Blake as he'd watched her. Was it possible she really was the source of all that raw need in him tonight? The idea that she might be sent a tremor of hope up her spine. If she was right, and Blake did want her that desperately, could she have been wrong about last night? He'd been warning her off almost from the start. Had his pretending to be asleep last night been his way of protecting her? Suddenly it all made perfect sense. It would be just like the hardheaded man to try to protect her from himself.

She heard a muffled swear from the den, then the sound

of Blake getting up and moving about. Her heartbeat quickened as she heard him coming down the hall. When he paused outside her door, Josie held her breath, hoping, wanting him to come to her. As impossible as it seemed, Blake did desire her. He even needed her. She'd read that desire and need in his eyes tonight, sensed it in the tense way he'd held his body. Maybe desire and need would be enough, she told herself, and waited for him to come into her room—to come to her. When he continued down the hall, disappointment hit her like a smack.

So what are you going to do, Josie? Bury your head under the pillow and cry?

She'd never been much on crying. She didn't want to be protected—not from the man that she loved. And she did love him, she admitted, seeing no point in denying the truth. Oh, she wouldn't lie to herself. She knew Blake didn't love her, that the two of them had no future together.

But there was now, her heart whispered.

And the man she loved needed her. Josie swung her legs over the side of the bed, then hesitated. What if he rejected her? Could her pride survive the rejection?

How much comfort will your pride be when he's gone?

Very little, she decided. At least this way she would help him feel less alone, and maybe in the process she would create her own memory. A memory to comfort her when he was no longer here. She reached for her robe, then decided against it. What was the point? He'd already seen her without it, and maybe…maybe it would be enough. Maybe she would be enough. Wearing only the pale blue satin gown, she grabbed the bottle of aspirin from her nightstand and started down the hall.

With her heart beating faster than a hummingbird's wings, Josie paused outside the bathroom. The door was slightly ajar, and she could hear water running inside. Scared, nerves rattling, for a moment she nearly ran back to her room. She didn't want to make a fool of herself. All she had was her pride. What if she lost that, too? Then she thought of the way Blake had looked—alone, lost, desperate, and she pushed open the door.

Blake stood in front of the porcelain sink, naked from the waist up, with his hands bracing both sides of the sink while he doused his head beneath the faucet. Shutting off the water, he heaved a deep sigh and lifted his head. Water streamed down his neck and face, while drops clung to a head of dark gold hair that looked like he'd raked his fingers through it one too many times. He buried his face in the ends of the towel draped around his neck. When he finished, he braced his hands on the sink again and stared into the mirror.

Lord, but he was beautiful, Josie thought, studying the sharp angles and planes of his face. The nearly two-weeks' worth of whiskers and the bandage on his forehead only added an edge of danger to his appearance. Her gaze met his in the mirror, and Josie's heart kicked against her ribs. His dark eyes were fixed on her, burning with a fire so intense she could almost feel the heat. His body had gone rigid and looked so unyielding that Josie thought surely if she touched him he would break.

He glared at the bottle of aspirin she held in her hand. "I said I didn't want any aspirin."

She heard the warning in his voice, but ignored it. "What about me, Blake? Do you want me?"

Desire flashed in his eyes, fire hot and lightning quick, before he snapped them shut. "Go back to bed, Josie," he commanded, his voice sandpaper rough.

"Come with me." Moving a step closer, she touched his shoulder. "Please."

Muscles tensed beneath her fingers, but she felt the shudder run through him. When he opened his eyes, they were wild, desperate. He looked like a drowning man going under for the third time. "You don't have a clue what you're inviting. Leave, Josie. Now! Go back to bed and forget about me. I told you. I'm bad news. I have nothing to offer you."

"I'm not asking you for anything, Blake. I'm the one of-fering." And her eyes never leaving his in the mirror, Josie offered him her love, her heart, her body. Unable to give him the words, she tried to show him. Opening the buttons of her gown, she let the blue satin fall to the floor. She stood naked behind him in the tiny bathroom, feeling more vulnerable, more exposed, than she had at any other time in her life. Emotions and nerves clogged in her throat. She wanted to cover herself, to turn off the light. But she didn't move. She could feel the burn of his eyes as he watched her in the mirror. The rigid line of his back echoed the strength of his control, but the hunger in his eyes gave her hope, gave her courage. Josie pressed her lips against his bare shoulder, and she tried to tell him with her kiss what was in her heart. That it was okay to need her. That she needed him, too. That she loved him. That she wanted him.

Swearing, Blake whipped around and caught her by the shoulders, his fingers biting into her bare flesh. Instinctively she clutched at his arms to keep her balance, and felt the coiled muscles, the ripcord power beneath the flesh. Josie stared up at him, took in the wet hair, the taut expression on his face, the soft mouth pulled into a forbidding frown. She held her breath, waited, feeling as though she were back on the top of that jungle gym again with the hard, cold ground waiting to greet her when she fell. Then she looked into Blake's eyes, and her fears vanished. A fierce storm of long-ing, of need, swirled in those dark eyes. No man had ever wanted her like Blake did. No man had ever needed her like Blake did.

And she had never loved anyone the way she loved him. She slid her hands up his arms, over his shoulders, looped them around his neck and pressed her mouth against his. At the touch of her lips, that end of the rope he'd been holding on to so tightly snapped.

He crushed her to him. "I'll probably burn in hell for this someday, but I don't care," he muttered. "I want you." Then he devoured her…with hungry kisses, demanding kisses, kisses that made her body ache, made her blood spin and set her on fire with need. When she thought she might surely go mad, his mouth softened, and he plotted a trail of gentle kisses, tender kisses, along her chin, her cheek, her eyes. The sweetness of those kisses proved equally shattering.

Josie grabbed his face between her hands and pulled his mouth down to her own. When his lips touched hers this time, the kiss was so gentle, so tender, so loving that she nearly wept. That he didn't love her, that she didn't have a prayer of building any kind of future with this man didn't matter. Not now. Not when she was in his arms, not when she could feel the beat of his heart next to hers. And she wanted. She wanted so much.

So she hugged him to her, ran her hands down his back to his hips, exploring all those muscles, the hardness of bone, the fevered skin. She hadn't known loving could be like this—this powerful, this huge, this wild. And she wanted all of it. She wanted all of him. Right here. Right now. She pressed her body against his, and showed him how much.

Blake tore his mouth free, gasped a breath. "Angel, slow down," he told her, a fevered look in his eyes.

Slow down? He wanted her to slow down when every nerve in her body said to hurry? Had she been wrong? "But I thought— Don't you want me?"

A growl came from deep in his throat. "Listen to me. Listen," he repeated. "I want you, angel. There's no question of that. But if we don't slow down, it's going to be over before we get started."

He kissed her again, and this time the room tilted beneath her feet. Josie grabbed on to Blake, and when he released her mouth she was in his arms, being carried down the hall to the bedroom. No one had ever held her like this before, made her feel like a beautiful princess, made her feel cherished. That Blake did so now made up for all those years of wishes that never came true.

He nudged open the door with his foot. The lamp she'd left burning sprayed a shower of gold light across the bed. Carefully, as though he thought she was made of glass and might break, Blake laid her down on the bed. Then he kissed her again. This time softly. Tenderly. Slowly. One gentle kiss spun into another and then another and another still, until Josie was no longer sure where one kiss ended and the next one began. And as the kisses lengthened, deepened, she could feel herself hurtling down a dangerous path.

Life had taught her how painful loving someone could be. She'd learned self-preservation early in life and knew to protect herself by never loving too much, never giving all of her heart, just a corner of it. Those warning bells were going off in her brain now, telling her not to love Blake too much, to only give him that corner of her heart that she could afford to lose. But her survival instincts were no match for the need and loneliness she tasted in Blake's kisses, that she felt in his touch. Instead of pulling back, she deepened the kiss and gave him all of her heart.

When Blake lifted his head and pushed himself up onto his elbows to stare down at her, Josie used the moment to look her fill. But looking wasn't enough. Not nearly enough. With a brazenness that should have shocked her, she reached out and touched him as she'd wanted to do from the first. She ran her fingertips down his shoulder over the fading bruise, traced a scar beneath his collarbone, followed the trail of deep gold hair down the center of his chest to his abdomen. When she hooked her thumbs inside the waistband of his pajama bottoms, he sucked in a breath. "Angel," he said, his voice desperate. "If you have any doubts, now's the time to say so. I'll understand," he told her. "I swear I will, and I won't blame you. You don't know who I am, what kind of man I am, what's in my past."

She pressed her fingers to his lips. "I know everything I need to know. You've shown me who and what you are in a hundred different ways already. You're the man I want.

The only man I want.'' Reaching for the pajama bottoms again, she paused, tipped her gaze back to his for a moment. ''Are we finished talking?''

He made a strangled sound in his throat and gasped when her fingers brushed his sex. ''We're definitely through talking,'' he told her. Stripping the bottoms off, he tossed them to the floor. Then he was moving over her, kissing her again.

Lord, but the man knew how to kiss, she thought, as he nibbled his way from her mouth to her jaw, to her ear. Then those skilled lips of his were teasing her breasts, with a flick of his tongue, with the barest scrape of teeth. And while he kissed her, his equally skilled hands were always touching her in some way—a lazy finger tracing the curve of her breast, a sweep of his hand along her rib cage, a tender stroke down her abdomen to the inside of her thighs. He had her so thoroughly aroused that by the time he eased a finger inside her, Josie nearly exploded. Wave after wave of sensation washed over her, tossed her about in a stormy sea of pleasure, and when she cried out his name he swallowed it with his mouth, and continued to hold her in his arms until the storm passed.

When she was able to focus again, Josie looked up into those dark eyes of his, caught the gleam in them just before he swooped down and started kissing her senseless again. But two could play this game, she thought. Before he could send her flying solo again, she shoved him onto his back and made a serious attempt to drive him out of his mind.

She took her time, learning his body. She discovered another scar where his appendix had been removed, a ticklish spot below his ribs, that the inside of his thigh was ultrasensitive. She'd never realized lovemaking could be this way, this beautiful, this giving.

''Josie,'' he said, his voice raspy. ''You've got to stop, honey. I don't have any protection in here. Let me go get my bag.''

She wasn't about to let him up—yet. ''We'll improvise,''

she promised and flicked her tongue down his hardened length.

The poor man nearly came unglued. "For Pete's sake, angel, you're about to drive me crazy!"

"That's the idea," she told him. Smiling, she circled him with her tongue, and proceeded to do just that.

Josie was driving him crazy, Blake admitted, several days later. The woman could almost make him believe his past didn't matter. Who and what he'd been before Josie didn't matter. Nothing mattered except being here with her and the twins, loving them, loving her. And he did love her, Blake admitted. He loved everything about Josie—from the way her eyes lit up when she was fussing over one of the twins, to the way she welcomed him into her bed and body at night. She was everything he wanted, everything he needed. And he wanted to be the man he was when he was with her, the man he was in her eyes. So why couldn't he shake the feeling that he had to find his past, that he had to finish whatever it was that he'd left undone? And why did he have a sinking feeling that when he did find his past, he would lose Josie?

"Isn't it wonderful?" Josie asked, breaking into his thoughts.

"What's that?"

She turned from the kitchen window, and her smile dazzled him. "The sun," she said, laughing. "I was beginning to think we'd never see it again."

He pushed away from the table and came up behind her to stare out the window. Because he needed to touch her, he circled his arms around her and pulled her back against him. The touch of her bottom had him hard in an instant. "You're right. It is wonderful."

"Blake," she said, shy surprise in her voice as he untucked her blouse. "It's not even noon and we...it's..."

"And it's been almost six hours since I've been inside you, angel. Not good for a man in my condition."

Her laughter turned into a sweet moan when he filled his hands with her breasts while he feasted on her neck. "A-and what condition is that?" she asked breathlessly.

"I'm an injured man. Remember?"

"Oh, yes. Your head. I almost forgot," she told him turning into his arms and reaching for the buttons of his shirt. "Want me to kiss it and make it better?" Capturing his face in her hands, she gave him a peck near the healing cut.

He frowned. "I'm still in a lot of pain."

"You are? Does it hurt here?" she asked, touching his mouth with her fingers. He nodded, and she kissed his mouth. When she finally lifted her head, desire churned in his blood. "Better?"

"Yeah, but I'm still hurting," he informed her, warming to the game.

"Really? Well, let's see. Does it hurt here?" she asked, dropping a kiss on his jaw, then another one at his throat. By the time she'd worked her way down his chest to his stomach, his body was on fire.

When she reached the snap of his jeans, her green eyes were pure devil as she looked up at him and asked, "Still hurting? Well, I wonder what I can do to help ease that pain?"

"Oh, I can think of a thing or two," he replied, then he went on to show her.

And later when she lay beneath him on the rug in front of the fireplace, and he was sheathed in her warmth, Blake knew he had never loved her more. As he lost himself in the sweet miracle of making love to Josie, he shut off the questions about himself, about his past. And when her body moved in rhythm with his, racing toward the center of another powerful storm, all of his thoughts and concerns about the past and the world beyond Josie's arms vanished.

Ten

Josie stood at the kitchen window and frowned at the sight of clear, blue skies and bright sunshine. The rain had stopped two days ago. The floodwaters that had isolated them at the farm had long since receded, and the roads had already been cleared of most of the debris from the storm. Even the temperatures had risen from frigid to cool, leaving just enough of a nip in the air to remind her that Thanksgiving was only two weeks away. And the beautiful weather had her as edgy as a long-tailed cat in a roomful of rocking chairs.

How was it possible for her life to have been turned upside down in the space of two weeks? The answer was simple—Blake. Looking back, she wasn't sure she'd ever stood a chance. She'd been a goner almost from the first time he'd called her angel. She loved him deeply, passionately and foolishly. Yet there had been times during the past few days when he'd held her and made love to her that she'd almost believed he loved her, too.

He didn't, of course. And while she might be a romantic

fool, she wasn't stupid. Blake might want her, even need her, but he would never love her. Not a man like him. Losing his memory had shaken him. He'd been a lost soul in need of someone to hold on to during an emotional storm, and she had happened to be the one there. She had no regrets on that score. She could never regret what they'd shared. But she had no illusions, either. His memory was coming back, in bits and fragments that sometimes disturbed him, but he was dealing with it. Soon he would be whole again, and when he was he would no longer need her. He would go back to the life he'd lost. Back to a life that didn't include her. Back to a life that included a woman more suited to him, a woman who was beautiful and special. Like him. She was neither. She was simply who she was—Josie. There wasn't a thing wrong with being ordinary. She was happy with who she was and what she'd made of herself. But being an orphan had taught her that when it came to relationships, she had to be a realist. She'd been passed over enough times to know that a man like Blake would never choose her. The last thing she was going to do, Josie promised herself, was make a fool of herself by trying to hold on to him. She'd play it light, play it easy.

"We're all set," Blake said from the doorway. "The munchkins are all strapped in, buckled up and ready to go. You about ready?"

One look at the man, and Josie's resolve turned to mush. There was nothing light and easy about the way he made her feel. She came up with a half-dozen reasons to cancel this trip into town. Then she shot every one of them down when she thought of the twins. They had to go, not just to arrange the tow of Blake's car, but to replenish the severely diminished supply of baby food and diapers.

"Josie? Honey, you all right?"

Pride, her only ally so often in life, came to her rescue now. She pasted a smile on her face. "Sure. I was just checking to see if we had everything we needed before hitting the road.''

Blake eyed her skeptically, then walked over to her, tipped up her chin. "You sure nothing's wrong?"

"Positive," she lied. "We'd better get going."

"In a minute. There's something I need first."

He kissed her. He rubbed his lips against hers gently, reverently, lovingly. When he lifted his head, Josie's knees all but sagged, and her heart felt ready to burst.

"You sure we need to go into town today?" he whispered, running his hand down her back to cup her bottom. "I can think of another way I'd like to spend the day with you. In fact, I've been thinking about the things I'd like to do with you from the moment I saw you in that skirt this morning."

Josie's pulse jumped at the look in his eyes. She was tempted, sorely tempted to give in to the sudden flare of desire sparked by his kiss. Oh, how she wanted him, loved making love with him. But when she reminded herself of Blake's needs and the needs of the twins, she knew her wants didn't matter. "Does that mean you're ready to deal with that alternative to disposable diapers that I mentioned earlier?"

The poor man went from lust to fear in a heartbeat. He caught her by the elbow and marched her toward the door. "You want to drive or should I?"

Blake drove. Instead of going to Royal, the closest town, she opted for Midland, which was in the opposite direction and a slightly longer drive. But it had been the direction from which Blake had been coming when he'd had the accident. Silently Josie admitted the other reason she'd chosen Midland was because she was still embarrassed over that crude drifter's 'sex-starved widow' remark in the Royal Diner. She suspected several people had overheard him, including that good-looking Forrest Cunningham. And while it was cowardly, she just couldn't face those people again now—especially with Blake. One look at her face, and they wouldn't have to wonder if she was still sex starved or not.

"There a particular reason you're squirming in your seat, angel?"

Josie's cheeks flamed.

"Never mind," he said laughing. "I think I can guess. Besides, we'll have to wait until we get home, anyway, since the town's right up ahead."

Josie's heart tightened at his reference to "home," and she immediately chided herself for reading anything into it.

"It's just about lunchtime, and I seemed to have worked up an appetite these past few days," Blake told her as they waited at a red light. "Do we have time to get something to eat? Or would you rather I arranged for the tow of my car and then have us hit the grocery store first?"

"Lunch sounds good to me," she told him.

"Then lunch it is."

Blake pulled into the parking lot of a diner and cut the truck's engine. By the time Josie unstrapped her seat belt and started to open the door, Blake was waiting for her. The gesture surprised her, touched her deeply. She wasn't used to having a man do nice, gentlemanly things for her, Josie admitted, as he took her hand and helped her down from the truck. That's why her heart got such a full, achy feeling now. Her feet touched the ground, but when Blake didn't release her, she tipped a glance up at him. The gleam in his eyes made her pulse sputter. Being the pirate he always reminded her of, he stole a kiss from her. And then he stole another, and another still, until he had her laughing and forgetting that he was only hers temporarily.

The fun mood lasted throughout lunch, where Blake had politely thanked the waitress who'd commented on their beautiful children. The remark had sent her romantic heart soaring like a bird and her head spinning with dreams. Oh, it was hard not to dream and fantasize with a man like Blake. He inspired dreams, had a way of making her believe those dreams could come true. Caught up in his festive mood, she allowed herself to pretend. That Blake would want to stay with her. That she and Blake and the twins could be a real family.

After arranging the tow of Blake's car, they headed to the supermarket. We're just like a family, Josie thought, as they laughed and joked while filling the shopping cart with baby essentials, food and indulgences. It pleased her beyond measure to discover Blake remembered her weakness for double-chocolate-fudge ice cream and to learn that he had a thing for oatmeal raisin cookies. By the time they reached the checkout line at the store, Josie couldn't ever remember being happier. She had everything she'd ever wanted right here, right now. Her heart full of love and hope that this time the dream wouldn't be snatched from her, she didn't feel ordinary at all. She felt special. She felt loved.

With her confidence running high, Josie picked up the razor Blake had thrown into their cart. "You know, Blake, I've been thinking," she teased, a smile curving her mouth. "I've kind of gotten used to that stubble of yours. How would you feel about growing a beard?"

When he didn't answer, she turned toward him, and the smile froze on her lips. Something was wrong. Seriously wrong, given the look on his face. "Blake, what is it?"

He didn't respond. His eyes remained locked on a tabloid he held clutched in his fists. She'd witnessed Blake in any number of moods these past two weeks—flirtatious and wicked, angry and frustrated, tender and loving. But never, never once during their time together had she seen him like this—so cold, so remote, so unfeeling. Josie moved beside him to see what had put that hard look in his eyes. Bracing herself, she read the headline, "Royalty in Texas?" She glanced at the photo of a dark-haired man, and stared into the coldest eyes she'd ever seen. Rubbing her hands up and down her arms, Josie read the smaller typeset, "Prince Ivan Striksky of Asterland, who recently announced his engage-

ment to Princess Anna von Oberland, was spotted in Royal
Texas...."

Confused, she shifted her gaze to the smaller photo—a
fuzzy inset of a beautiful blond-haired woman in a gorgeous
gown. Suddenly dread fisted in Josie's stomach. Even in the
blurry photograph the woman was breathtaking, and exactly
the type of woman she could see with Blake. She glanced
down at her own denim skirt, plain blouse and boots. She
didn't need a mirror to know that comparing herself to the
princess was like comparing an alley cat to a Persian. Her
throat tight, Josie forced herself to ask, "Blake, please. Tell
me what's wrong."

"I just remembered who I am. My name's Blake Hunt."

The coldness in his expression as he looked at her had the
blood in Josie's veins turning to ice. She took note of the
princess's blond hair again and forced herself to ask him
"And the twins?"

"Are not mine. I kidnapped them."

All through the drive home and even as he gave Josie the
bare facts about the death of the twins' mother, about Prince
Ivan's plans to use them to gain control of Princess Anna's
country by forcing her into marriage, about the Alpha Team's
rescue mission, formed by select members of Royal's exclusive Texas Cattleman's Club, uppermost in Blake's mind
were the mistakes he'd made with Josie. Had it not been for
the amnesia, he never would have allowed himself to become
involved with her. Damn it! What was he going to do? Since
he and Lily had ended their engagement years ago, he'd
taken care to avoid relationships like this one, relationships
where there was emotional risk. The women he chose to be
with were like him—they had nothing to give, wanted nothing from him in return.

But Josie was different. She was the kind of woman who
stole a man's heart piece by piece with her shy desire and
explosive passion, with her sweet warmth and stubborn pride

with her generous heart and fierce independence. Damn it! He was in love with her, and he had no right to be. He certainly didn't deserve her love. And though she'd never told him, he knew damn well that she was in love with him. He'd even let it happen. And he shouldn't have. He was bad news, just as he'd told her. He'd seen too much, done too much. He had too little to give, too little to offer, and if he stayed with her, he would make her life hell. He couldn't do that. What he could do, what he would have to do, was tell her the truth.

"I'm sorry about the interruptions," she said, returning to the den and taking a seat at the opposite end of the sofa from him. "They've finally settled down. Please go on, tell me the rest of the story."

"There's not a whole lot more to tell. As I explained, because of my military training, I was the one assigned to get the twins out of Asterland and bring them back to Royal and reunite them with their aunt."

"Princess Anna von Oberland."

"Yes. She became their legal guardian when her sister, Edward and Miranda's mother, died."

"She's very beautiful," Josie told him, her gaze straying to the photo in the tabloid that lay on the coffee table.

"Yeah. I guess she is. I know my brother Greg certainly thinks so."

Josie tipped her gaze up to his. "Your brother?"

"Greg." Blake thought about his brother and remembered the look that had come into the other man's eyes when he'd spoken of the princess at the start of the mission. "Greg's never said anything, but I get the feeling there's some history between the two of them. Greg has been protecting Anna and her son. I'm sure her picture getting splashed across this tabloid makes things dicey. But Greg will deal with it."

"I see," Josie replied.

But she didn't see, Blake suspected. She didn't see that he didn't care a fig about Anna or how beautiful she was. It was

Josie who was the real beauty as far as he was concerned because her beauty came from within. It shone in her eyes in her smile, in the way she loved. And it was Josie he loved Only he had a job that didn't allow for a normal life, that didn't allow for a woman to share his life. How could he love her and ask her to share such a life with him? He couldn't. But, he wanted to. Badly.

"So what happens now?"

He explained the rest of the details of the mission and the part that each of the five members of Alpha had played. "I'll need your promise not to repeat anything I've told you. Outside of the men involved and the princess, no one know about our mission."

"You don't need to worry. I won't say anything."

"I'll need to use your phone again to contact my brothe so I can make arrangements to take the twins to their aunt.'

"Yes, of course," she said standing. "I need to check on them, anyway."

When Josie left the room, Blake reached for the phone. A he punched out the private number to his brother's home, he thought about leaving here, about leaving Josie. Just the ide of doing so left an acid taste in his mouth and an ache in hi chest. For the first time in his life he envied his brother' home in Pine Valley, Royal's exclusive residential area, an Greg's steady job as an attorney. Had he chosen a differen path, were he to alter that path now, he wouldn't have t walk away from Josie. But how did he walk away from wh he was? The things he'd done? He didn't, Blake admitte and if Josie really knew the man he was, she wouldn't war him. It was better this way, he told himself, as the phon began to ring on the other end. Leaving his job wasn't a option. Unfortunately, asking Josie to be a part of his lif wasn't an option, either.

"This is Hunt."

"Greg, it's Blake."

"Blake! Where in the hell are you?"

"At a farmhouse about two hours outside of Royal."

"A farm? What are you doing on a farm? And where in the devil are the twins?"

Blake explained about the car accident, his amnesia and Josie. In turn, Greg confirmed what Blake had read in the newspaper about Prince Ivan being spotted in Texas. What Blake hadn't realized was that Princess Anna had gone into hiding in plain sight as a waitress at the Royal Diner. From the sound of things, the arrangement had more than rattled his big brother, and Blake wondered if he had been right in his early perception that there was something more than friendship between his brother and the princess.

"There's more," Greg told him, and from his brother's somber tone of voice, Blake suspected it wasn't good news. "I have someone tailing Striksky. They managed to bug the hotel suite he was staying in last week."

"And?"

"And it wasn't good. The bastard's furious that his plans have been thwarted. His not being able to find Anna and William or you and the twins have pushed him to the edge. The guy's crazy, Blake, and he's out for blood—yours. You need to be careful."

"I can take care of myself. What about Anna? Are she and William safe?"

"They're safe," Greg told him, steel in his voice. "Striksky will have to go through me to get them. You're the one I'm worried about. You and the twins."

"You think he'd hurt those babies?" Blake asked, angered by the very thought.

"I think the man's unstable enough that it wouldn't matter to him who he hurts as long as he manages to destroy you."

"He won't get the chance," Blake assured Greg. "And if he so much as harms a hair on those little guys' heads, his country will be looking for a new ruler."

When he hung up the phone a few minutes later for Greg to take another call, Blake thought again about leaving here,

about leaving Josie. The thought of doing so grew more dis
tasteful and more painful by the minute.

"Did you reach your brother?"

Blake glanced up to find Josie standing in the doorway
holding Miranda. "Yes. He had an urgent fax coming
through. I hope you don't mind, I gave him the number here
to reach me."

"Of course not. I wasn't sure when you'd be leaving.
mean you're welcome to stay as long as you like to, but I'm
sure the princess is anxious to see Miranda and Edward."
She hugged Miranda close, buried her face against the baby'
head. "I'm going to miss them so much."

And me? he wanted to ask. *Will you miss me, too, angel*

The phone rang. "Go ahead and answer it. That's probably
your brother."

It was his brother, calling back to tell him that the crisis
was over. Greg had received a fax from an attorney handling
the estate of the horse trainer killed in the accident with Prin
cess Anna's sister. The man, who had apparently worked fo
Prince Ivan, had among his effects a signed agreement be
tween the prince and himself, in which the trainer had re
nounced his rights as Miranda and Edward's father i
exchange for money.

"So what happens to Miranda and Edward now?" Josie
asked when he explained the situation to her that evening
after dinner. "Will the princess take them back to Obers
bourg with her?"

"Not according to my brother. He's heard through the
grapevine that Anna is going to find a family to adopt them."

"But I don't understand," Josie replied, her eyes wide
with disbelief. "I know the princess must love them very
much or she never would have gone to so much trouble to
rescue them."

"She does love them. If she's really decided to give them
up for adoption, it must be because she wants a better life
for them, a happier life than what she and her sister, Sara

had. It couldn't have been easy growing up the way they
did—bound by royal traditions of the monarchy, with parents
who put their duty to the throne above their children's wel-
fare.''

''Funny, isn't it? How when we're kids we think how
lucky it would be if we could be a princess or a prince? It
doesn't sound like Princess Anna's sister was lucky or very
happy.''

''From what I understand, she wasn't. And I don't think
Princess Anna is, either.'' Blake paused, considered her com-
ments and wondered. ''Is that what you wanted to be when
you were growing up, Josie? Did you want to be a princess?''

''Sure. All little girls do, I guess. I even made up my own
fairy tale about it.''

''Tell me.''

She hesitated, then her eyes took on a glazed look as she
stared at the logs burning in the fireplace. ''When I was little,
I used to dream that this big white car would drive through
the gates of the orphanage and stop right out in front. Then
the door would open and this beautiful lady and very handsome man would get out of the car. They'd walk up the steps
of the home and knock on the door and ask to see the direc-
tor. Then they would tell her that they were a king and queen
and were here looking for their little girl, who was actually
a princess and had been stolen from them. They would describe the missing princess. She had green eyes and long
black hair, and her name was Jocelyn, but they called her
Josie. Princess Josie.''

Blake's throat grew tight as he imagined a young Josie, a
lonely little girl yearning to be loved, to be wanted. ''Then
what would happen?''

''Then all of the girls at the home would line up so they
could be inspected. The king and queen would walk down
the line, shaking their head as they passed girl after girl. Even
the most beautiful little girls with blond curls and big blue
eyes would be passed over. Finally, they would come to me,

and the moment they saw me, they would start to smile. 'That's her,' the queen would say. 'That's our Princess Josie.' And then they would hold open their arms and hug me close as though they never ever wanted to let me go. Then I would be whisked away in the beautiful white car and taken to a big beautiful castle, where all my brothers and sisters, who were also princes and princesses, of course, were waiting to welcome me home.''

Unable to resist, Blake went to her. A fist squeezing around his heart, he tipped her face so she would look at him. ''If I were a prince, Josie, I'd whisk you away to my castle right now, and I'd never, ever let you go.'' And then he kissed her, with all the love and longing in his heart.

He'd meant to only kiss her once. But he should have known kissing her once wouldn't be enough. No way could he kiss her mouth and ignore the long line of her throat. And how could he kiss her throat and ignore the pale skin at the vee of her blouse? And there was simply no way he could ignore the puckering nipples of her breasts that strained beneath her bra. Unbuttoning her blouse, he unclipped her bra and after filling his hands with those breasts, he washed the deep rosy tips with his tongue.

Josie arched her back, whispering, ''Make love to me, Blake. Make love to me.''

He wanted to make love to her, but knew he didn't deserve to—not when he had nothing to offer her, not when he had to leave her. He would just kiss her, pleasure her, and not take, this time, he promised himself. He could do it. All it took was a little self-control. He had plenty of self-control, Blake reminded himself. In fact, he prided himself on that. Lives depended on his being able to keep his head, and he'd long ago mastered control of his body, his needs, his desires. Easing Josie down onto the couch, he slid his hand up her legs and inside her panties to the center of her sweet heat.

She lifted herself up against his hand. When he touched her and she shuddered her release, he swallowed her gasp with his mouth, wanting to give to her, to show her how much she meant to him. She tore her mouth free, her hands flying to the snap of his jeans. "No, angel," he told her. "This is for you. Just for you."

"But I want you," she said, and brushed her fingers against his sex. Her touch shook his control badly. Still, he resisted. Then she looked into his eyes, her angel's eyes gleaming with passion, with love. "Blake, please."

The sweet plea in her voice, the yearning in her eyes, obliterated his so-called control. Within seconds she had him free and protected, and was guiding him to her heat. Shaking with the need to be a part of her, he thrust into her in one swift, hard stroke before he could stop himself. "Josie," he gasped. "Angel, did I hurt you?"

"No," she told him, and when he started to withdraw, she tightened her female muscles around him. He thought he would faint from the pleasure and pain of it. He wanted to go slow, make this good for her. But the lady had other ideas. Easing herself up, she managed to roll him onto his back. And then she was sitting astride him. Her hair had long since escaped the prison of her braid and hung in a mass of wild black silk down her breasts, her back. She reminded him of a goddess, wild and wanton as she tested him, rode him, pushing him harder, farther. He nipped at her breasts with his teeth, laved them with his tongue. She tasted like roses, like rain, like magic, he thought.

And then suddenly he couldn't think at all because Josie was calling out his name, and he was clutching at her hips, rising to meet her hurried thrusts. And with each thrust she took them closer and closer toward some impossibly high cliff. Then he was the one crying out her name as they both tumbled off the edge together.

Later that night, and into the morning hours, as he held Josie in his arms, he wondered how in the world he had managed to survive all these years without her. And how in

the world was he going to survive all the years to come
without her?

"How am I suppose to survive for the next two hour
without you to help me?" Blake asked Josie the next morn
ing as she read off a list of instructions for him regarding the
twins.

"You'll do just fine, Blake. So will they."

But he didn't miss the sadness in her voice, the pain be
neath the fake smile. His angel never could lie worth spit
She was hurting. And he was the cause. "Josie, I'm sorry.
wish things could be different."

"What would you make different, Blake? Would you take
away these past few weeks we've had together? Would you
take away what we shared last night?"

"No."

"Neither would I." She tipped up her chin, and met his
eyes bravely. "Even if I could, I wouldn't take back one
minute of it. Not one."

He slid his arms around her. "I wish I were a different
man, a man with a normal job, a normal life, a man who
could promise you a future. If I could, Josie, I would. But
can't. I can't offer you any of those things."

"I don't recall asking you to offer me anything, Blake.
never expected anything from you two weeks ago, and
don't expect anything now. If that's why you think I made
love with you, then you were wrong."

"What I think is that you made love with me because
you're in love with me."

Her eyes glittered with anger, with hurt, with pride. "So
what's your point?"

"The point is that I love you, too."

She went absolutely still. Her eyes were hot, but her skin
was ice-cold. "I know there's a *but* here somewhere, Blake.
So why don't you just say it, and then you can be on your
way."

Her response both shamed him and angered him, because it was true. "I'm trying to do the right thing here. I love you. Too much to mess up your life by asking you to be a part of mine."

"I see. So you love me, but you're leaving me for my own good. Do I have that right?"

He ignored her sarcasm. "I've tried to tell you about my job, about the agency I work for. The type of work that I do—it isn't pretty. It isn't something I can share with you, with anyone. I've seen things, done things, things that if you knew about, you'd run as far and as fast from me as you could."

"I doubt that."

"Do you, angel? Do you really? See these hands?" He held them up in front of her to inspect. "These hands have killed men. And not by accident and not always on a battle-field. It doesn't matter that the lives of the men I took were evil, that their deaths were justified or that by killing them I saved innocent lives. What matters is that I'm the one who killed them. And more than likely, I'll kill again. Even if I wanted to get out of the agency, to retire, to make a life with you, I couldn't. There are too many people who would suffer if I wasn't there to do my job when I was needed."

"Why are you telling me all this? Do you think you'll shock me or disgust me? Is that what you want?"

"What I want is for you to understand why I can't be with you. Why I can't ask you to marry me. I learned a long time ago that loving someone isn't always enough."

"A lesson no doubt you learned from Lily."

"Yes. We were engaged, but she couldn't handle what I did. It ripped her up to know what I was capable of."

"She sounds like a wimp. If you ask me, you were lucky she dumped you."

"Maybe I was, but I learned a lesson. That you don't sub-ject a woman you care about to that kind of life."

"Then I guess it's a good thing you're not asking me to marry you, Blake, because I'd have to turn you down."

"I know." He'd expected as much, yet he felt as though she'd kicked him in the teeth.

"Oh, not because of all that malarkey about your job. Any woman who loved you wouldn't want to change you and she wouldn't expect you to change for her. She'd accept you and your job as part of who you are, what you are and learn to deal with it. I would never marry you because you're not really in love with me."

Blake was still reeling from her comeback, wondering if maybe he had been wrong, if maybe he did have a chance to make a life with Josie. It took him a moment for the rest of her words to register. "I'm not?"

"No, you're not. You have a noble streak a mile long, Blake Hunt, and you're grateful to me because I was here when you needed someone to hold on to, because I helped you through a bad time. But any fool can see I'm not the kind of woman you'd fall in love with. I'm not the kind of woman you belong with."

Furious with her for saying such a thing, for not realizing how special she was, Blake retorted, "And do tell me, Ms. Walters. Just what kind of woman do you think I'd fall in love with? What kind of woman do I belong with?"

"A woman who's elegant and beautiful, who wears designer dresses and has a family she can trace back to Plymouth Rock. A woman who belongs at parties where you entertain princesses and politicians. A woman who's special like you are. I'm not that woman, Blake. I never could be."

But, oh, how she wished she were that woman, Josie thought an hour later, as she finally convinced Blake to go. She watched as he and the twins drove away from the farmhouse and out of her life. When she walked back inside, the house had never seemed so empty. And she had never felt so alone in her life.

She was still feeling empty and alone two days later when, after discovering one of Miranda's socks, she called the apartment that Greg had set up for Princess Anna and her son. "Thank you for taking my call, Princess, and for letting me know how they're doing."

"Please, call me Anna. And I was happy to hear from you. I wanted a chance to thank you for taking such good care of my niece and nephew."

"I was happy to do it, Prin—Anna."

"Oh, by the way, Blake just arrived to see the twins. Did you wish to speak to him?"

Josie wanted to shout yes, but instead she said, "No. But thank you."

"It's probably just as well that you don't speak to him now. I expect the accident and rescuing the twins has taken its toll on him."

Josie's heart nearly stopped. "Is he...is Blake all right? I mean, he isn't ill, is he?"

"No, not in the way you mean. His body is well, but I don't think his heart is." She paused. "Forgive me, Josie. We do not know each other, but I thought perhaps you were the cause."

"Me? You're mistaken, Anna. I couldn't be the cause." Unwilling to allow hope to take root, she decided to end the conversation. "I really do need to go. But thank you again for speaking to me, and please, give Miranda and Edward each a kiss for me. I hope..." Josie swallowed past the lump in her throat. "I hope you find a good family for them."

"As a matter of fact, I have the perfect couple in mind," Anna told her.

Hanging up the phone, Josie swiped at the tears on her cheeks. Her heart aching, she wondered how long it would be before the twins and Blake forgot her, and if she would ever be able to forget them.

She wasn't ever going to be able to forget them, Josie decided the next week as she drove back from Midland and passed the spot in the road where she had rescued Blake and the twins. Rethinking those frantic moments of driving through the storm with them, she turned off the highway onto the road to her farm. And then she saw it. A big, beautiful white limousine parked in front of her house. Her heart racing, Josie gripped the steering wheel with both hands and started down the drive. Before she had stopped the truck, the door of the limo opened, and Blake got out.

Her fingers shook as she switched off the engine. Afraid to let herself hope, Josie simply sat there, drinking in the sight of him. He'd lost weight. There was a scar on his forehead now instead of a bandage, but he was the most beautiful sight in the world to her.

He pulled open the door to her truck, tipped back his hat to look at her. "You going to hide in there the rest of the day, angel?"

"I wasn't hiding."

He arched a brow in that cocky way only he could do and held out his arms to help her down.

She didn't trust herself to touch him. So she said, "I can manage."

"Yeah. But I can't." He reached up and pulled her out of the truck and into his arms.

"Blake! What do you think you're doing? I—"

He cut off her protest with his mouth. There was hunger in his kiss. And desperation. And something she'd never witnessed in him before—fear. When he lifted his head, he said, "I love you. If I were the noble and good man you think I am, I would leave you right now and let you find someone who deserves you. But I'm not noble and I'm not good. And I'm not going to leave you to find someone else, because I don't want to live without you. I'm no prince, and I don't have a castle to offer you as a home, but I love you, and I need you."

"Oh, Blake—"

"Please, angel. Let me get all of this out while I can. My job—it won't be as big a problem as before. I've talked to my superiors, and while I'll still do some traveling, it won't be as much. I can't get out completely—at least not yet— but I won't be required out in the field the way I have been. And if you'll agree to marry me, to take a chance on me, I swear I'll spend the rest of my life trying to become the kind of man you want me to be."

"Oh, Blake." She caught his face between her hands. "You don't have to become the man I want. You are the man I want. You always were." And this time she kissed him, tried to show how much she loved and needed him.

Josie was so lost in the joy of kissing Blake, it took a moment before she registered the sound. She jerked her mouth free. "What was that?"

"What was what?" he asked, already kissing her neck.

"Crying." She shoved at his shoulders. "Blake, I heard a baby crying."

"Oh, Lord. Hurry, before the other one starts," he said, and started dragging her with him back to the limo.

"The other one?" she repeated.

"Dammit! We're too late," he told her, diving inside the backseat. He came out holding a crying baby Edward.

"Eddie!" Josie squealed and took the crying baby, whose little arms were reaching for her already.

Blake dove back inside and came out with Miranda. "Hey, it's all right, sugar britches."

"But I don't understand. What are they doing with you?"

A flush colored his cheeks. "I brought them along as re-inforcements."

"Reinforcements? But I don't understand. Princess Anna said she'd found a couple to adopt them."

The flush deepened. "Um, actually, we're the couple."

Josie felt shocked. Overwhelmed. Delighted. "Us? You and me?"

"I sort of got used to the idea of being their dad, of us being a family."

"So did I," Josie admitted, kissing Edward's fingers.

"I knew I loved you and wanted to marry you the morning I left here."

"Then why didn't you call, Blake? Why didn't you come back?" Josie asked.

"Because I had to complete my mission and turn these two over to Anna. I needed to make sure she would be willing to let us adopt them. And I wanted to give you some time away from me to think about the things I'd said. But everything took longer than I'd planned, and by the time I was able to come back and tell you, I wasn't sure if you loved me enough to take a chance on me. So I brought these two monsters along because I knew how much you loved them, and I thought you might take me if I used them as a bribe, " he confessed.

"You didn't ever need to bribe me, Blake."

"So, what's your answer, Princess Josie? Will you marry me? Will you marry us? Spend the rest of your life with us?"

"Yes," she cried out, her heart bursting with joy, with love. "Oh, yes!" She kissed Blake. She kissed Miranda. She kissed Edward. And then she kissed Blake again, and at last Josie realized she'd found her home.

Epilogue

Blake kissed his wife again in front of all of his family and the close friends who'd gathered at the Texas Cattleman's Club for a combined celebration of their recent wedding and the christening of their son and daughter. At the familiar ping against his head and the laughter that followed, Blake ended the kiss. "Hank, old buddy, I think you'd better have a talk with your future club member over there about the inappropriateness of throwing objects at other club members."

Hank Langley, grandson of the club's founder, looked at the twins being held by Blake's parents and then back at Blake. He arched one dark brow. "I don't know, Blake. Can't say I blame Edward. If Josie were my mother, and you kept kissing her at the drop of a hat, I'd probably shoot you with a pacifier, too."

Everyone laughed—including Blake himself. He skimmed the crowd of well-wishers once more for sight of his brother, and when his gaze met Princess Anna's in inquiry, she shook her head. Deciding he shouldn't wait any longer, he lifted his glass. "Ladies, gentlemen, friends. I'd like to propose a Thanksgiving toast. To all of you here tonight, my dearest friends and family, who honor me with your friendship and love. To the two newest blessings in my life—my children, Edward and Miranda—who make me want to be a better man. And to my beautiful wife, Josie," he said, his eyes seeking hers, "who, because she loves me, enables me to be a better man. Never has one man been as truly blessed."

"Hear! Hear!"

Blake clinked his glass to Josie's and smiled at his wife, his love, as applause erupted around them.

"Blake. Josie. Congratulations," Hank Langley's wife, Callie, said, kissing them each on the cheek. Within moments a line formed behind them of people waiting to offer their good wishes.

"You didn't waste any time," Sterling Churchill commented, giving him a slap on the back.

"Talk about working fast. Looks as if I'm not the only one who's going to be answering to Daddy," Blake said, teasingly. "What I don't understand is how you got Susan here to marry you when she wouldn't even look at me twice?"

"Oh, I looked," the former librarian informed him, a twinkle in her brown eyes. "I just wasn't buying." She turned to Josie and hugged her. "Congratulations. I'm hoping our children will get to be friends, and that you and I will be, too."

"I'd like that very much," Josie told her.

"Congratulations, Blake, Josie," Forrest Cunningham said, his arm tucked around his own new bride.

"Surprised?" Becky Cunningham asked, her smile as sassy as her red hair.

"Not me," Blake informed the couple. "I knew from the time you were a flat-chested brat in pigtails trailing after this ugly cowboy that you were going to be the woman to end his bachelor days."

"Did you now?" the former Becky Sullivan said. "Then I wish you'd have told Woody here and saved him all the trouble of dating half the females in Texas."

"Yes, Blake. Why didn't you?" Josie all but purred.

Laughing, he continued to accept congratulations and good wishes from friends, and then he spied his brother Greg entering the ballroom. Blake couldn't help but notice how his brother's gaze immediately sought out Princess Anna and how quickly he was at her side. From Greg's somber expression and the sudden pallor of Anna's skin, Blake knew something was wrong. "About time you showed up, big brother."

"Sorry I'm late. The sheriff has a roadblock set up along the lake, and I had some trouble getting through."

Blake's eyes narrowed. No way would his brother have let something like a roadblock delay him. Instincts, honed in hundreds of covert operations, told him the news wasn't pleasant. A signal from his brother had Blake excusing himself and Josie from their guests. And after being assured that his parents would look after the twins, he and Josie escaped down the hall of the club to a private room.

He entered the room and found Langley, Churchill, Cunningham and his brother gathered around an ashen-faced Anna. Josie went immediately to Anna and urged her to sit down.

"What's happened?" Blake asked, cutting through the tension.

Greg's eyes met Anna's again. "A man was spotted jumping off the bridge earlier. The sheriff and his deputies searched the lake for his body."

Josie gasped beside him, and Blake held her close. "Do they know who it was?" his wife asked.

"Yes," Greg replied. "It was Prince Ivan Striksky. His body was recovered a few minutes ago. He left a note, confessing to his sins where Princess Anna and her sister were concerned. He apologized for bringing shame upon his country and felt he couldn't face his people.''

The room became a buzz of voices, of questions. "Blake," Josie said, tugging at his sleeve. "Look at Anna's face."

As he looked, the relief gave way to sadness in the princess's dark green eyes. "Come on, love," Blake said and steered his wife closer to the Princess.

"Anna, I'm so sorry," Josie said. "This must be very difficult for you."

"Yes. It is," the Princess replied softly. "I still find it impossible to believe he's really dead, that he is no longer a threat to me and my son."

"Now that Skriksky is gone, does this mean…are you having second thoughts about your decision to allow Blake and me to adopt Edward and Miranda?" Bracing himself, Blake held Josie close and waited for Anna's answer.

Anna's eyes widened, and she looked from Josie's face to his and back again. "No. No second thoughts at all," she assured them. "I will miss them. But I know that they could not be in better hands. You are just the family my sister would have wanted for them."

He could feel some of the tension ease in Josie. "Then what's wrong? Why are you so…so sad?"

"Am I that obvious?" she asked.

Josie took the other woman's hands. "Only to someone who has known what it's like to feel sad and alone."

Feeling a little uncomfortable at the woman talk, Blake considered excusing himself to join his brother who was in a circle with fellow Cattleman's Club members, Hank Langley, Sterling Churchill and Forrest Cunningham. But he couldn't help notice the way Greg's gaze kept straying to Anna as though he was reluctant to let her out of his sight. A man who had recently fallen under the spell of a woman himself, Blake recognized the possessive gleam in his brother's eyes. *Well what do you know?* Blake thought. *Looks like big brother Greg is about to take the fall.*

"You are right, of course," a still-stunned Anna told Josie. "I...I am sad. I suppose...I suppose it's just that with Ivan—" she paused, tried to steady herself as if she still hadn't digested the full impact of his death "—with Ivan no longer a threat, I really have no reason to stay in Texas."

A smile curving his lips, Blake turned his attention from his brother to Anna. "Oh, I wouldn't be so sure about that," he murmured under his breath. "In fact, if I were Anna, I wouldn't pack my bags just yet."

*   *   *   *   *

In the exciting conclusion to the
TEXAS CATTLEMAN'S CLUB
miniseries, find out what happens when
Princess Anna von Oberland and Gregory Hunt
finally reunite their lost love...
in their explosive story

LONE STAR PRINCE

by Cindy Gerrard
Coming to you from Silhouette Desire
in December 1999.

And now for a sneak preview of

LONE STAR PRINCE,

please turn the page.

Hollywood couldn't have staged a more dicey plot. An evil prince. A beautiful princess in his clutches. A midnight rescue by an ex-Marine and ex-lover, come charging in to save the day.

Trouble was, this wasn't Hollywood. It was all too real, and as Greg Hunt stared grimly across the cabin of the private jet bound for the States, he hadn't yet decided if he was the hero or the chump in this little melodrama.

The woman gazing vacantly out the window of the starboard side of the aircraft was exhausted, but still, her bearing was regal, her posture erect. Four years ago when Greg had first met her she'd been beautiful. There was no denying she was beautiful still. Yet Princess Anna von Oberland, loved by the paparazzi, adored by the masses, had been robbed of the wide-eyed innocence that had struck him as both intriguing and irresistible those many years ago. A haunted, hunted edge had painted pale violet smudges beneath her summergreen eyes, drawn fine lines of tension around a smile that was forced and shallow and reserved only for the child sleeping at her side. Her silk-and-velvet voice, with its honeyed, husky resonance, spoke of lost summers and faded dreams and hinted at her European lineage only when she was exhausted. As she was now.

Shifting uneasily, Greg took his own turn staring out the window into the blackness of night at thirty-one thousand feet. He tried to divorce himself from an unrelenting need to hold her. Seeing her like this—seeing her again—had brought back feelings he'd thought were dead and buried. And while he was relieved she had turned to him for help— he was prepared to do whatever it took to protect her—he was also determined not to let her or her solemn-eyed little boy breach the wall he'd built around his emotions when she'd walked away from him four years ago.

Determined, but unfortunately not 100 percent successful, he admitted grudgingly as, against all resolve not to, his mind wandered back to the summer night they'd first met. He'd been a Marine on his last tour of duty and on leave in the little European principality of Obersbourg. She'd been a princess on the run from her family, her obligations and the stark reality of her position in life.

It seemed like a lifetime ago that their eyes had met, locked, held across a street full of dancers in the plaza. A lifetime since they'd woven their way unerringly through the crowd and into each other's arms. Since they'd danced. Fallen in love. Made love. Parted.

He quickly checked the memory. There was no point hashing that over again. It had been four years. He'd put it all behind him—at least he had until he'd received her transatlantic call last week, and the panicked sound of her voice had brought it all back as though it was yesterday.

Gregory. I need you. Please come. Please...come.

So he had. With the backing of Texas billionaire Hank Langley and Langley's Avenger—a Hunt Industries aircraft—the able assistance of Sterling Churchill and Forrest Cunningham, all members of Langley's Texas Cattleman's Club, they'd smuggled the princess and her son out from under the Obersbourg royal guard not three hours ago.

He scrubbed the back of his knuckles absently against the stubble of his jaw and stared broodily into the dark. Damned if he knew why he'd been so ready to let himself get wrapped up in her life again. He only knew that this time it wasn't by chance. This time there was more at stake than reckless hearts and stolen moments. He didn't have all the details sorted out, but he knew that Anna's sister, Sara, and Sara's lover were dead, the victims of a mysterious car crash. Sara's infant twins were in the physical custody of Ivan Striksky, the playboy prince of Asterland, who was holding them the equivalent of political hostages as part of a plot to force Anna to marry him. And Greg, it seemed, had been cast in the role of White Knight.

White Knight, hell, he thought as the hushed whispers of Churchill and Cunningham—men he'd been glad to have guarding his back—drifted from the aft end of the Avenger. This little caper had "international incident" written all over it. It was going to take a damn sight more than his law degree to smooth some very ruffled, very royal European feathers when this thing broke wide open and the king and queen of Obersbourg discovered their golden goose was missing.

He stretched his long legs out in front of him, figuring he'd deal with it when it happened. In the meantime the only part he had left to play in this little scenario was to see Anna safely to the States. She was a resourceful woman; she'd figure out where to go from there. All he needed to do was get on with his life—and quit thinking about why this woman, above all women, could mess up his head in more ways than he could catalog or name.

If you enjoyed what you just read,
then we've got an offer you can't resist!

Take 2 bestselling love stories FREE!

Plus get a FREE surprise gift!

Don't miss Silhouette's newest cross-line promotion,

Four royal sisters find their own Prince Charmings as they embark on separate journeys to find their missing brother, the Crown Prince!

Royally Wed

The search begins in October 1999 and continues through February 2000:

On sale October 1999: **A ROYAL BABY ON THE WAY**
by award-winning author **Susan Mallery** (Special Edition)

On sale November 1999: **UNDERCOVER PRINCESS**
by bestselling author **Suzanne Brockmann** (Intimate Moments)

On sale December 1999: **THE PRINCESS'S WHITE KNIGHT**
by popular author **Carla Cassidy** (Romance)

On sale January 2000: **THE PREGNANT PRINCESS**
by rising star **Anne Marie Winston** (Desire)

On sale February 2000: **MAN...MERCENARY...MONARCH**
by top-notch talent **Joan Elliott Pickart** (Special Edition)

ROYALLY WED
Only in—
SILHOUETTE BOOKS

Available at your favorite retail outlet.

Visit us at www.romance.net

SSERW

Start celebrating Silhouette's 20th anniversary
with these 4 special titles by
New York Times **bestselling authors**

Fire and Rain
by Elizabeth Lowell

King of the Castle
by Heather Graham Pozzessere

State Secrets
by Linda Lael Miller

Paint Me Rainbows
by Fern Michaels

On sale in December 1999

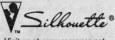

In December 1999
three spectacular authors invite you to share the
romance of the season as three special gifts are

Delivered by Christmas

A heartwarming holiday anthology featuring

BLUEBIRD WINTER
by *New York Times* bestselling author
Linda Howard

A baby is about to be born on the side of the road. The single
mother's only hope rests in the strong arms of a dashing doctor....

And two brand-new stories:

THE GIFT OF JOY
by national bestselling author **Joan Hohl**

A bride was not what a Texas-Ranger-turned-rancher was
expecting for the holidays. Will his quest for a home lead to love?

A CHRISTMAS TO TREASURE
by award-winning author **Sandra Steffen**

A daddy is all two children want for Christmas. And the
handsome man upstairs may be just the hero their mommy needs!

Give yourself the gift of romance in
this special holiday collection!

Available at your favorite retail outlet.

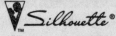

Visit us at www.romance.net   PSDBC

SILHOUETTE®
Desire®

continues the captivating series from
bestselling author **Maureen Child**

BACHELOR
BATTALION

Defending their country is their duty;
love and marriage is their reward!

December 1999: **MARINE UNDER THE MISTLETOE**
(SD#1258)

It took only one look for Marie Santini to fall head over heels for
marine sergeant Davis Garvey. But Davis didn't know if he was
capable of loving anyone. Could a Christmas miracle show him the
true meaning of love?
